BOOKS BY SCOTT CORBETT

The Trick Books

The Lemonade Trick
The Mailbox Trick
The Disappearing Dog Trick
The Baseball Trick
The Turnabout Trick
The Hairy Horror Trick
The Home Run Trick
The Hockey Trick
The Black Mask Trick
The Hangman's Ghost Trick

Suspense Stories

Cop's Kid
Tree House Island
Dead Man's Light
Cutlass Island
One by Sea
The Baseball Bargain
The Mystery Man
Dead Before Docking
Run for the Money
The Case of the Gone Goose
The Case of the Fugitive Firebug
The Case of the Ticklish Tooth
The Case of the Silver Skull
The Case of the Burgled Blessing Box
Grave Doubts

Easy-to-Read Adventures

Dr. Merlin's Magic Shop
The Great Custard Pie Panic
The Boy Who Walked on Air
The Foolish Dinosaur Fiasco
The Mysterious Zetabet
The Great McGoniggle's Gray Ghost
The Great McGoniggle's Key Play
The Great McGoniggle Rides Shotgun
The Great McGoniggle Switches Pitches

What Makes It Work?

What Makes a Car Go?
What Makes TV Work?
What Makes a Light Go On?
What Makes a Plane Fly?
What Makes a Boat Float?

Ghost Stories

The Red Room Riddle
Here Lies the Body
Captain Butcher's Body

Nonfiction for Older Readers

Home Computers: A Simple and
  Informative Guide

Grave

Doubts

Grave

Doubts

by
Scott Corbett

Joy Street Books
Little, Brown and Company
Boston   Toronto   London

10 9 8 7 6 5 4

Library of Congress Cataloging in Publication Data

Corbett, Scott.
  Grave doubts.

  Summary: Two sixteen-year-old boys, suspicious
of the sudden death of an eccentric millionaire,
look for a clue to the mystery in the last crossword
puzzle the old man worked on.
  [1. Mystery and detective stories] I. Title.
PZ7.C79938Gn 1982   [Fic]   82–10050
ISBN 0–316–15659–0

*Joy Street Books are published
by Little, Brown and Company (Inc.)*

BP

BOOK DESIGNED BY S. M. SHERMAN

*Published simultaneously in Canada
by Little, Brown & Company (Canada) Limited*

PRINTED IN THE UNITED STATES OF AMERICA

To Mary and Dick
Philbrick

Grave

Doubts

1

SLOW DOWN! WE'RE NOT DUE for fifteen minutes!"

Wally Brenner had taken off **down** the sidewalk in that bustling strut that was his usual gait. He stopped, and looked around impatiently.

"So what? It could rain any minute. Listen to that thunder!"

"I know you. Curiosity is killing you," I said as we started down Salem Road more or less at my pace. "By now you've thought of seventeen reasons why Mr. Canby wants to see us tonight, all of them wrong."

"Well, if Hobby knew, he sure wasn't saying. How did you like the way he looked when he told us?" Wally went into a purse-lipped, prune-face imitation of Shapley Hobson. " 'I advise you to be

3

prompt. I can assure you I intend to be, though I'm not scheduled until nine o'clock.' "

"I especially liked the way he said 'scheduled.' I guess your dad's right — Mr. Canby and Hobby must hate each other's guts."

"Well, Mr. Canby was a hotshot stockbroker in Boston when Hobby was the youngest bank president Adamsport ever had — and Dad says Mr. Canby always called him a small-time hick. Mr. Canby wasn't always straight in all his dealings, but Hobby was. Anyway, they had some real run-ins, I guess."

And time hadn't changed their feelings any, even though by now Mr. Canby was old and ailing, and Mr. Hobson had taken early retirement from his bank in order to devote himself to the restoration of Adamsport Village, as the old waterfront section of town was now called.

The Canby house was only about four blocks from Wally's, at the corner of Salem and Old Farm Road. It was one of the oldest and finest Colonial frame houses in town outside of the Village area. We'd been taking care of the grounds for the past three years, and knew it well. As we cut across the side yard, we stopped to cast a professional glance around us.

"Okay, all you grass blades!" I said. "Tomorrow you're gonna get it!"

"Yep." Wally was sizing up the old house.

4

"Imagine moving that thing all the way to the Village! It's going to be something to watch."

Mr. Canby had announced some time ago that he was planning to leave the house to the Adamsport Village Association. For Shapley Hobson that had been the most exciting news of the year.

"Well, Hobby may not like Mr. Canby, but I guess he's ready to do just about anything to get the house for the Village."

"That's right, Les — even if it means putting up with us."

We had Mr. Canby to thank for our brand-new summer jobs at the Village. He'd ordered Hobby to take us on. We were to mow, weed, plant, trim, and so on, and although we considered ourselves landscape gardeners Hobby considered us groundskeepers.

I checked my watch. We still had almost ten minutes to wait. A car came around the corner and turned into the drive.

"Now, who's that?"

"Can't be Hobby. Too early."

It was cloudy and nearly dark, but we could see the man who got out of the car well enough to recognize him. Of course, it helped that we'd heard he was back in town.

He rang the doorbell with a flourish. When the door opened, the light from inside made his shiny black mustache look as if it were pasted on his plump, smooth face. He boomed out a big good evening and went inside.

"Well, whaddya know?" said Wally. "Otis Fournier. Must be at least a year since the last time he showed up."

"Just about. Remember how mad Victor was when he met him coming out of the house? I thought Victor was going to flatten him."

"I guess they both wish their uncle had one less relative. How would you like to be the nephew of an old gent who's worth millions?"

"I'd want to be the *only* one, that's for sure."

"Well, at least they don't have any other competition. They're the only relatives he has left."

"Sure — but they'd both like to have it all." Wally was in his element. He loved intrigue. "So tonight it's going to be Otis and us and Hobby. What's Mr. Canby up to?"

"Could be an interesting evening."

We made sure we rang the bell at 8:45 sharp. Kevin Murphy let us in. Kevin and his wife Agnes had been taking care of Mr. Canby for the past five years. None of us could understand how they could put up with him so meekly and uncomplainingly.

"Hi, Kevin."

"Good evening, boys."

His tone was glum, and so was his jowly face, and it was not hard to guess why. Like a lot of peo-

6

ple, he took a dim view of Otis the Prodigal Nephew.

"Follow me," he said, and led the way upstairs on large flat feet. The air in the house was close and smelled like medicine Being there was a strange experience for us, because in the months since Mr. Canby had become an invalid we had never seen him except once in a while at his window.

From the bedroom at the end of the second-floor hall came sounds of rich, buttery laughter and the croaking, wheezing noises that were all that was left of Mr. Canby's laugh.

"You study that list, Otis," the old man was saying. "They're valuable. You'll find one of them is very valuable, when the time comes, especially after you work *this* out. Let's see how good you really are at puzzles!"

Puzzles? What kind of puzzles? And what was valuable? Wally glanced back at me and lifted his eyebrows. It was already an interesting evening.

Kevin paused in the doorway.

"The boys are here, sir."

"Send them in."

Mr. Canby was slowly writing something in a small paperback book, or I should say printing something, rather than writing; you could tell that from the stiff movements of his pencil. Intent on what he was doing, he didn't look up right away, which was just as well. It gave us a chance to get over the shock of seeing him. He had always been a thin, scraggly man, but now he looked wasted away to the bone. He waved a skeleton hand at two straight-backed chairs, and his smile, with its big teeth and drawn-back lips, changed his face into a death's head.

We tried not to look surprised at Mr. Canby's appearance and said good evening just as he said, "Oh, before you sit down, shake hands with my nephew Otis. You'll be seeing a lot of him, especially if you keep working at the Village. Otis, this is Lester Cunningham and Wally Brenner."

Otis Fournier was spread all over a black leather-upholstered armchair beside the bed, and he was looking at the papers his uncle had just handed him. As we stepped toward him, he glanced up and smiled.

"Certainly I remember the boys. You were working in the yard the last time I visited here. And you're still keeping the old place looking its best!" His dark button eyes twinkled at us, totally friendly, and I could see how his uncle might find him likable despite all the messes he'd gotten into. "How are you, boys?"

He leaned forward to stretch out his hand to us and dropped a couple of pages of the papers he was holding. Wally was quick to retrieve them for him, but managed to drop one of the pages himself. As he reached for it he held the others at a natural angle that just happened to give me a good look at them, and in the meantime he was having a second chance at the page he had dropped. A typical Wally Brenner maneuver. He only took a few seconds, and did it all very well. When he had returned them to Otis, we each shook his soft and rather clammy hand and said it was nice to see him again.

Mr. Canby's bedroom was a treasure-house of old-fashioned interior decoration. Nineteenth-century steel engravings and a couple of family portraits, all fairly dismal except for some seascapes, covered up a lot of the busy Victorian wallpaper. A four-poster of sturdy oak dominated the room. A rolltop desk and swivel chair were against one wall. The rolltop was up. Papers bulged out of it in an untidy mess. A bedside table top was littered with medicine bottles and pillboxes.

Mr. Canby chatted with us, asking us how we liked our work at the Village, taking a couple of sly digs at our new boss in the process. Meanwhile, Otis had an eager eye on the paperback his uncle was holding.

"Uncle Otis, could I see that book?" he asked finally.

"Oh! Sure." Mr. Canby handed it to him with a chuckle. "Here — let's see how good you are. Here's the answer, now work out the clue. I was going to leave it with the list in a letter for Ernie Beemis to give you after I was gone, but I'd rather have the fun of seeing you sweat it out now. If you're half as good at crosswords as I think you are. you won't have too much trouble."

During the next few minutes, while Mr. Canby was talking to us, Otis sat staring hard at the page where the magic word was written.

Just for fun I kept a discreet eye on my watch. Sure enough, at nine on the dot, the doorbell rang.

"There he is!" Mr. Canby laughed, and his expression changed. His eyes took on a mean glitter. He gestured impatiently at Otis. "Put that book aside for now, Otis — I don't want you to miss any of this. Stick it in the end pigeonhole. I always keep my current crossword book there," he added with an old man's fussy precision.

After a moment Kevin appeared again in the doorway.

"Mr. Hobson is here, sir."

"Well, by all means, show him in!" cried Mr. Canby. "Make way, Kevin, make way!"

2

SHAPLEY HOBSON WAS SMALL, short, slim — a mere wisp of a man, you might have said, except that wispy people don't have steely eyes and rigid backbones. The steely eyes flicked around the room and he did not pretend to smile.

"Right on the dot as always, Shapley. Welcome, welcome! You remember Otis, of course," Mr. Canby went on, as Otis struggled to his feet.

"Good evening, Otis." Hobby went through the handshake without noticeable pleasure.

"Good to see you, Shapley," rumbled Otis with automatic affability. He sprawled in his armchair again, while Hobby sat down ramrod-stiff in an uncomfortable-looking armchair.

"I won't keep you long, Shapley — just a couple of things I wanted to go over, but important things.

Yes, sir, mighty important," he said, winking broadly at Otis, who beamed back at him. There was nothing subtle about Mr. Canby's brand of kidding. "First of all, Shapley, there's the matter of Missy's room."

His wife had died twenty years ago. Her room adjoined his, with a connecting door that had been kept shut since her death, as was the room's other door into the hallway. Twenty years, and in all that time no one had been allowed to enter the room except Mr. Canby himself and the various people who had cleaned the room every spring and fall under his watchful eyes.

"Of course, you know my stipulations concerning her room, Shapley. Nothing touched, nothing moved, everything to stay exactly as she left it."

Hobby nodded, and recited his formula.

"When the house is moved to the Village and tours are taken through it, the hall door will be open so that visitors can look into the room, but it will be cordoned off with a silk rope so that no one can enter."

"Kee-rect, Shapley. But now, you know, we don't have an exact inventory of what's in there, and I've decided I want to see one before I die, so that I can add any notes of interest about the contents that may occur to me."

For the first time Hobby relaxed a little. He was always eager for additional information about anything exhibited in the Village. Where history, especially local history, was concerned, he was a fanatic.

"An excellent idea! I'll be glad to make the inventory myself."

"I was going to ask you to do so, Shapley — but with a little help. That's why I wanted the boys to be here tonight."

His chuckle, deep and croupy, was not pleasant to listen to, but at least he enjoyed it. He fixed Hobby with a malicious grin, alert now to his every reaction, waiting to savor his discomfort.

"You know what an old crook I am, Shapley, and being an old crook I know how to keep other people honest. Now, if you were to go into that room and do an inventory all alone, even a model of uprightness like yourself, what with your interest in old things, might be tempted beyond his strength to start picking up things for a closer examination, or opening bureau drawers, and so on. Even two people might not be safe — but it's hard for three not to keep each other honest. So — just to please a poor dying man — I want the three of you to do the inventory together. You can describe the items in the room, and the boys can take it all down. All right?"

Now we understood why we were there. For one reason only — to make the situation all the more humiliating for Hobby; to have us sitting there when he was told we were being appointed to keep him honest. I could imagine what must have been going through his mind. "How much more of this am I going to take? . . . Still, he probably is a dying man, he can't last much longer, and then . . ." I suddenly found myself wondering if Mr. Canby had been the kind of kid who enjoyed pulling wings off flies. For all of an occasional bark or snarl, he had always been pretty decent to Wally and me. This was a side of him we had heard about but had not seen.

When Hobby spoke, he managed to restrict himself to two words, though he almost choked on those.

"Very well."

"Spoken like a trouper, Shapley! An old trouper, a really good actor," croaked Mr. Canby, relishing his rather nasty triumph. And then he made his face go solemn again. "Now, the other matter, and then you may go — I'm sure you have other things to do tonight, Shapley."

"I'm in no hurry."

"Good, good! Well, then. As you see, my nephew Otis has come home to Adamsport once again — at my request — and this time he's here for good. He admits he's tired of drifting all over the country — the world, even! — and I'm going to make it attractive for him to stay here now and assume his rightful place in Adamsport. Tomorrow when that stick-in-the-mud lawyer of mine gets here I'm going to make it very attractive for him to stay here."

The room was so still that when Mr. Canby paused, as much to catch his breath as anything, we could almost hear tomorrow's Fat Cat Otis Fournier purring in his armchair. A lifetime of discipline was keeping Shapley Hobson's face frozen in place.

"Now, Otis has had his faults, we all know that — you know you have, you rascal!" said Mr. Canby, waving an indulgent finger while Otis chuckled and tried to look sheepish, "but one good thing he does have is a feeling for the family, for its history, for its accomplishments, and for this house and the things in it. So one of the projects I want him to take on, now that he's back in Adamsport to stay, is this . . ."

Mr. Canby's eyes seemed to glow as he lifted himself away from his pillows, a scarecrow in pajamas, and looked straight at Shapley Hobson.

"I'm going to name Otis to be curator of Canby House when it's moved to the Village."

If Mr. Canby wanted to make Hobby miserable, this was a master stroke. Hobby's hands were small, but the way they were gripping the arms of his chair I expected the wood to splinter. His face was livid, blue-white, leaden, almost as deathly as Mr. Canby's.

"But — but — none of the houses or buildings have separate curators! I cannot be expected to administer the Village properly if there are to be autonomous organizations within it!"

"Now, now, Shapley, don't take on so. I only feel I want to have a member of the family involved."

"I'm sure we can work together just fine, Shapley," said Otis Fournier. "I have a few ideas about the whole setup, but I'm sure there's nothing we can't . . ."

His words trailed off as Hobby turned a flame-thrower of a look his way, but Otis's uncle took up where he had left off.

"I feel the family should be involved, and that's that," he said in a hard tone of voice.

Hobby stood up.

"Very well. Is that all?"

"Oh, now, don't rush off, Shapley, I thought you weren't in a hurry, and I was thinking of saying to hell with doctor's orders and having a drink to celebrate this happy occasion — oh, but you don't drink, do you?" With Mr. Canby, there was no letting up. "Go ahead, Shapley, and sleep on it. By morning I'm sure you'll have decided it's better to have the house in the Village on my terms than not to have it at all."

Hobby gave him a stiff nod, and the same to Otis.

"Good night," he said, and left the room. Mr. Canby watched him go. He chuckled again, loudly enough to make sure Hobby heard him. Then as he glanced at us his face smoothed out into something more human.

"Mind you make a good job of that inventory, boys!"

"Yes, sir!"

"And don't take too much guff off of . . ." Grinning, he tilted his head and jerked a bony thumb toward the door. We were sitting with our mouths open, and our astonishment obviously amused him. Obviously, too, it never occurred to him we might find his performance disagreeable.

"Yes, sir. Goodnight. Goodnight, Mr. Fournier."

We got out as quickly as we could and scuttled down the hall. From the head of the stairs we could see Hobby and the Murphys standing close together, talking in low tones. They looked like conspirators.

". . . intolerable for all of us!"

Whatever Hobby was saying, that much reached us before any of them noticed us. They stepped apart as we came down. We said hello to Agnes and got a worried nod. Hobby and Kevin exchanged a look, and Kevin opened the door. Hobby's eyes went on to Agnes, and he said, "Well, goodnight to you both."

"Goodnight, sir."

We said goodnight and followed Hobby outside. When the door shut behind us, I found I couldn't keep my mouth shut. I had to say what was on my mind.

"That was pretty rotten, sir."

I took Hobby by surprise. At first he tried to be displeased, but then he sort of broke down into a human being and looked grateful.

"It wasn't pleasant," he admitted. He glanced up at the house, and we could see his lean face working. "To think such a house has to come to the Village from a man I —"

Once more his habitual prudence took over as he left the thought unfinished. Then the silence was broken by the sweet sound of a motorbike swooping past along Old Farm Road.

"There goes Dinky Davis," said Wally admiringly, while Hobby stiffened with indignation.

"Motorcycles! Noisy, pesky things — they should be banned!"

"Dinky's is pretty quiet, sir. You ought to hear some of them "

"I've heard them. I not only detest them, I recently wrote a strong letter to the newspaper about them."

"Oh, sure, I remember," said Wally. "My dad read it to us." He also remembered, as I did, how we'd all had a good laugh over it. Needless to say, Wally and I took a different view of motorbikes than Hobby did.

"Well, goodnight, boys. I'll see you in the morning."

Hobby climbed into his car and drove away. Wally and I looked at each other and laughed.

"Well, what say we take the trail back, Les?"

We walked around the house to pick up the trail that ran through the woods. Before we took off, though, we stopped to look back at the old house. All the rear windows were black, but in the darkness, light from somewhere shimmered dimly on the paint and gave it a red-black sheen. Somewhere in the distance, but closer now, thunder rolled like a muffled drum. For no good reason, I shivered.

"Why does that kind of thunder always sound like a warning?" I wondered

3

THE TRAIL RAN THROUGH THE woods behind Salem Road all the way to Boxwood Avenue near the Edgewood Motel. We knew every inch of it, even in the dark.

"Otis Fournier!" I shook my head. "Now, there's a real addition to the top brass at the Village."

"You know what I think Mr. Canby's up to? He's using Otis to try and get rid of Hobby! He wants to make him mad enough to quit."

"He won't quit. He might do a lot of things, but he won't quit."

"Right. But listen, what about that list? From what I could tell, it was a list of pictures Mr. Canby had written out."

I nodded.

"His own pictures, I think. You gave me a pretty good look!"

"I tried to."

"I could read something about a ship picture painted in Hong Kong Harbor."

"*Fishing Boats in the North Sea* and a harbor scene were on the sheet I dropped. Did you take a good look afterwards at the pictures in the room?"

"Every chance I got."

"So did I."

"One of them could be a ship in Hong Kong Harbor."

"Yeah, I know the one you mean, the one over the desk. It's a real ship's portrait, the kind those port artists painted, not just a general scene."

"The ship I saw listed was *Grey Hunter*, and the captain was a Canby. I got that much."

"I wish we knew what Mr. Canby wrote in that puzzle book!"

"So do I, Wally. There was some connection, that's for sure. And one thing we know is, Mr. Canby's a real puzzle freak. You've heard Kevin and Agnes talk about it. And look at some of the stuff he's pulled on us! Remember the time he said he wouldn't pay us off the next day unless we could give him a word with three double letters in a row?"

"Bookkeeper." Wally nodded. "But he made the

word he wrote down for Otis sound pretty important."

"Well, I guess we'll just have to ask Otis. After all, we'll be seeing a lot of him now."

"Maybe. And of course we've got another treat in store, too. Doing the inventory with Hobby. That really burned him up."

We had reached the spot where a well-worn path turned off toward Wally's backyard.

"Coming in?"

"No, I'd better go home and shut some windows before it rains. See you at breakfast."

Somehow I didn't feel like helping Wally tell his folks about all that had gone on — not that he would need any help. I just wanted to sit around and think about it by myself.

Since my parents were away at a convention I was eating all my meals at the Brenners'. When I walked in the next morning thinking about Mrs. Brenner's good pancakes I wasn't ready for the news that greeted me. Wally didn't look at all like his usual self. He was tense and serious.

"Did you hear?"

"Hear what?"

"Mr. Canby's dead."

The words sounded crazy, unreal. Mr. Canby dead? Otis Canby, whom we had seen and spoken to less than ten hours ago — how could he be dead?

And while this shocker blazed in my mind, some other thoughts, wild possibilities, zeroed in like tracer bullets.

"I can't believe it! How did it happen?"

"Who knows?"

I glanced out the windows, and pointed.

"I'll bet he knows!"

Wally's Uncle Matt was coming up the front walk. He walked in looking as if he hadn't had much sleep. Wally's father, J.G., said, "Morning, Matt! What happened to old Canby?"

"He died."

"I know that! But how?"

"Give me time. I need a cup of Edna's coffee."

"Have you been to the house?"

"Yes."

Matt Brenner was Adamsport's chief of police. He was one of those ruddy-faced gray-haired men who look like everybody's uncle from the sticks. He managed to fool a lot of people with that look, people who didn't realize until too late that the bumpkin façade hid a razor-sharp mind.

He was also eating his meals at the Brenners', because his wife was in Syracuse visiting her sister. I had known him all my life, and was privileged to call him Uncle Matt, too. As he headed for the kitchen he glanced our way.

"I hear you squirts were there last night. Come tell me about it."

While he ate ravenously and drank two cups of coffee, we told him about our visit. He listened without comment and with total concentration. By the time we finished he was sitting back over his third cup of coffee.

"Those Murphys," he said. "They're no fools. They called a doctor first, but then just to be on the safe side they called me. Got my number through the station and called me at home."

"What do you mean, 'just to be on the safe side'?" J.G. sat forward, scenting mystery. Wally came by his curiosity honestly — got it from his father. "How did he die?"

"Give me time and I'll tell you," growled Uncle Matt. It was an old refrain — J.G. interrupting with questions, Uncle Matt telling things in his own deliberate way. He turned to us. "After Hobson and you boys left, the old man was in high spirits. He ordered Murphy to bring drinks and cigars and then leave him and Otis alone. There was a lot of laughing and joking — the Murphys admitted they were worried enough to keep tabs on what went on — and the men even worked on a crossword puzzle together. Seems that's one thing they had in common, they were both puzzle nuts.

"The Murphys heard some funny things. Once they heard a jingling sound, and Canby said, 'Take good care of these, they could be the keys to your happiness!'"

"Keys to the house, probably," said J.G. "If he was going to be curator —"

"Yes," said Wally, "but why —?"

"Another time he said, 'You've got the list and the magic word, and I expect the answer by morning or you're no puzzle whiz!' Otis said, 'How do you know I haven't already got it, Uncle?' and with that they both laughed, and it sounded as if Otis poured another round of drinks. All this carousing went on till after eleven o'clock before Otis finally left.

"A few minutes later the Murphys were getting Canby settled for the night. They'd just given him his medicine and tucked the covers in around him when all of a sudden he sat up, let out a terrible groan, and grabbed his chest. He said, 'Otis!' and fell back on his pillows. They called Dr. Schmidt and he came right over, but there was nothing to be done. Canby was dead."

Bang. There it was. Drama. Mystery. Death. And this was for real. For a moment nobody spoke.

Then J.G. said, "Well! I don't blame them for calling you."

"Those drinks!" said Wally. "Did Otis poison his uncle's —"

"Or put something in his cigar?" I said. "If the cigar butts are gone I'd be pretty suspicious!"

"Now, hold it!" Uncle Matt held up his hand like a traffic cop. "We'll wait for the autopsy report. I don't think there's any foul play involved at all.

Don't you squirts start talking this up like it was some murder mystery on TV! Why would Otis do a crazy thing like poisoning his uncle? Unless there's something we don't know, he had nothing to gain and plenty to lose. I went over to the Edgewood, where he's staying, and broke the news. He was in his pajamas, having a nightcap. He seemed bowled over. When I told him his uncle had called out his name just before he died, Otis looked startled, but I can't say he looked concerned."

"All that money . . ." mused J.G. "I suppose Victor Ridgway will get most of it now."

Victor and Otis were the same age, in their forties. Mr. Canby's two sisters had died years ago, each leaving one son. Victor was a widower with no children. Otis had never married. Victor was in the construction business, and lived on the Canby property in a modern number he built himself, not far from the Canby house. Some people said he had spent his life trying to keep on the good side of his uncle and crowd his cousin out of the picture, and Otis had certainly done everything he could to make the job easier. Estimates ran high as to how many times Mr. Canby had taken Otis out of his will, only to put him back in later — because he couldn't help liking Otis. And on the other hand, he couldn't seem to make himself like Victor very much.

Meanwhile, Wally was thinking about something else.

26

"You said they'd just given him his medicine, Uncle Matt . . ."

"That's right. Some pills he took every night. Dr. Schmidt was still there when I got there. He told me just what they were, and said they might not have been doing Canby much good but they certainly wouldn't have killed him. So don't start working yourself up about that!"

We did no more speculating in Uncle Matt's presence, but plenty as we biked to work.

"Okay, Les, is it Otis or the Murphys?"

"The Murphys."

"Come on!"

"Well, look at the opportunity they had! Were those last pills Mr. Canby took his regular pills, or something else?"

"In other words, they could poison Mr. Canby and pin the crime on Otis? But why, Les? What would be in it for them? I can't see them even thinking up such a scheme."

"Someone else could do their thinking for them."

I had allowed the dark thought that was in both our minds to surface. We were looking down the staircase again and hearing Hobby say, ". . . intolerable for all of us!" There seemed to be some sort of understanding between Hobby and the Murphys. Could it be that a word was passed, an order given . . . ?

"Well, I remember Uncle Matt's saying that some of the most coldblooded murderers have been ordinary old couples you wouldn't think would hurt a fly," said Wally.

"And fanatics like Hobby . . . I mean, his whole world is the Village now. . . ."

"What could Kevin and Agnes have at stake? Well, who knows? They could have reasons for feeling threatened by the changes Mr. Canby was talking about. And listen, how about Victor? Is there any way he could have pulled a fast one?"

"Now, that's a thought. The Murphys have always run to him for everything. They don't draw a breath without Victor's okay. And they don't like Otis."

Whenever anything needed fixing at the house it was Victor whom Kevin called, and it was Victor who either sent someone to do the fixing or came by and fixed it himself. Because they were useful, Victor had always treated the Murphys pretty well.

"The Murphys let him know that Otis was back in town and coming to see his uncle last night. After we left they phoned him again and told him Mr. Canby was planning to change his will today. So Victor said, 'He mustn't live till morning.' How's that for a scenario?"

" 'We'll wait for the autopsy report,' " I said, doing a passable imitation of Uncle Matt.

By now we were passing the Canby house. I slowed down to look at it and try to realize that Mr. Canby was not there anymore. Suddenly Wally swerved into Old Farm Road and motioned me to follow.

"Hey, where you going?"

"I just thought of something, something that won't wait."

He pulled over. I stopped alongside.

"What?"

"I want to see that puzzle book. I want to get hold of it before someone else does."

"How are you going to do that?"

"I think I must have dropped my pocket knife on the floor up in Mr. Canby's room after I showed it to him last night," he said with a straight face. "You know — this one."

He pulled out the Swiss Army knife Mr. Canby had given him for Christmas.

"Why, you conniving so-and-so, you don't think Kevin will let you go up and look for it, do you? You know him — that room will be Off Limits."

"I know. He'll probably insist on going up with us, but that's where you come in. While he's watching me look for the knife, you're going to grab the book."

"What? Now, wait a minute —"

"Don't worry, I'll get him to turn his back."

"But —"

"Listen, don't you want to know what the magic word was?"

"Yes, but —"

"All right, then, let's go! If we hurry we can still get to work on time."

In most ways I was not like Wally at all. I was tall and skinny, and inclined to fall into relaxed positions when not busy. I preferred to stay out of trouble, rather than look for it. Yet I constantly let myself be tempted by my curious, conniving busy-body of a buddy into situations that could mean all kinds of trouble. Now that I thought about it, I *did* want to know what that word was. I was hooked. But what if I bungled my part? Suppose Kevin saw me grab the book?

Naturally, the whole business made me mad, especially my inability to say no.

"Fine, fine! Sure, let's go," I snarled, wheeling my bike toward the house. "If anything goes wrong we'll only lose our jobs when Hobby hears about it, and our skins when Uncle Matt finds out."

But, as I say, while I was letting off all this steam I was wheeling my bike toward the house. Wally grinned.

"You worry too much, Les. We'll pull it off smooth as silk. I'd let you do my part while I grabbed the book, except that I'm better at conning people than you are."

"That's for sure!"

We went around back and rang the bell. The window curtains twitched. Then the door opened.

"Morning, Agnes!"

"Morning, boys. I was afraid it might be one of those reporters or somebody. Come in."

Agnes was a small, meek-looking woman, but not as meek as she looked. She did a pretty good job of bossing Kevin.

"Hi, Kevin."

From his chair at the kitchen table Kevin nodded to us over his morning newspaper.

"Gee, it was hard to believe the news this morning," said Wally. "It must have been a terrible shock to you two."

No one would have doubted it from the look of them. Their faces were drawn, they were dead beat. They exchanged a troubled look. Kevin nodded again.

"It was indeed."

"Gave us a turn, too — what with seeing him just last night, and all. Well, anyway, we stopped by because I think I dropped my knife up there. You didn't find it, did you?"

"A knife? No."

"You know, it was Mr. Canby's Christmas present. I thought he'd like to know I always carried it with me, so I showed it to him last night, and now it's gone. I could have dropped it on the carpet and not noticed, so — Mind if I go up and take a look?"

True to form, Kevin raised objections.

"Well, now, I'm sure you didn't lose it there, because we tidied things up after — after poor Mr. Canby had been taken away and everybody had left, and certainly your knife didn't turn up."

"I was sitting near the bed, it could have rolled under."

"Oh, take him up and let him look, Kevin," said Agnes.

Kevin sighed.

"Very well." He gave in without being very gracious about it, and motioned us to follow. "But I'm sure you won't find your knife up there."

So far, so good. But then when we walked into the bedroom our hopes sank, because the top had been rolled down on the desk. It was almost shut.

Wally still had to go through the motions, of course. While Kevin and I watched, he got down on his knees, lifted the end of the bedspread, and stuck his head under it. After a moment he pulled his head out and said, "Well, you're right, Kevin. It's not here."

"You see, Wally, I knew we couldn't have missed it, not something that size," he said in a kindlier tone, now that he'd had his small triumph, and turned to lead the way back downstairs, with Wally right behind him shooting a glance at me and jerking his head toward the desk.

"Well, when Agnes said you hadn't found it I knew there wasn't much chance," he told Kevin, "but now I'm worried, because I can't imagine where I lost it . . ."

As their voices receded down the stairs, Light-fingered Lester was easing up the rolltop, sweating for fear it would squeak — as it did, but not much. I only rolled it up enough to shove my arm inside and feel around for the right-hand pigeonhole. My fingers closed on what felt like the spine of a paperback —

"Lester! Where's Lester?"

My absence had been noted.

"Be right with you!" I called as I eased down the rolltop. But heavy flat footsteps were already coming up the stairs, and they sounded like angry footsteps. I had flouted authority.

What I had felt was a paperback, and the paperback was a puzzle book. I jammed it deep into my hip pocket, reached into my side pocket, dropped to my knees, and stuck my head under the bed about a second before Kevin came in.

"Lester, what do you think you're doing?"

I pulled my head out.

"Just taking a look myself. Wally, you need glasses," I said, and held up a Swiss Army knife.

4

W ELL, WHADDYA KNOW?"
Wally grabbed the knife happily. "Where was it?"

"Behind the leg. I'll admit it wasn't easy to see."

Kevin looked annoyed. He didn't like being wrong.

"Of course, we don't expect to have to look under the bed every time we tidy up. Come along, now, I've other things to do!"

We got on our bikes and rode for two blocks before Wally stopped to give me back my knife. He had been grinning ever since we walked out of the house.

"Not bad, Les," he said. "You're showing promise."

"Survival," I growled. "Pure survival. Good

thing you didn't say we both carry them all the time."

"You got the book?"

"Sure."

"I could tell by your smug expression. Let's stop and see what the magic word is!"

"No! We're almost late now."

"You've got a point. We ought to be on the dot when we walk in on Hobby."

"Do what?"

"Well, I've been thinking. I want to see him while the news is fresh. Why shouldn't we? After all, we were at the house together last night, and . . ."

"And the autopsy report isn't in yet, is that what you mean?"

Adamsport Village clustered around Front Street, which curved along the waterfront to the old lighthouse at Scudder Point. Many of the old buildings such as a shipwright's shop, a rope walk, a ship chandlery, and a shipyard had survived, and others — a ship carver's shop, a sail loft, and an apothecary's shop — had been moved there from other loations.

The most important exhibits, however, were the ships and boats. An old square-rigged training ship lay at Long Wharf and a Gloucester fishing schooner at Fish Dock. North Wharf had a packet boat nearly a hundred years old. And besides these we had twenty kinds of small craft around the place: all the catboats, pinky schooners, whaleboats, and dories people got about in locally before there were such things as outboard motors — or decent roads.

The whole Village was fenced in, with two entrances for the paying customers. Admissions provided about two-thirds of the bankroll needed to keep the place going, with public support and a few grants providing the rest. Shapley Hobson not only drew no salary, he was a big contributor to the project himself. It was his whole life now.

The administration offices were in a handsome brick house of the late Georgian period, built in 1820 according to our official guidebook. Hobby's second-floor office looked out over the Village green that was one of the areas we were responsible for keeping spic and span. Since the receptionist wasn't at her desk yet, we had a clear shot at Hobby.

His door was open. He was busy at his desk. When he looked up and saw us he did not seem surprised. The sharp eyes behind his rimless glasses and the set of his thin lips gave nothing away about his feelings.

"Come in. I see you've heard the news," he said, reading our faces correctly. "I suppose everybody has. I won't play the hypocrite with you, I didn't shed any tears, but at the same time it's always something of a wrench when a town loses one of its oldest and most prominent citizens. He was the last of the Canbys; the last of that name, at any rate."

Wally went on a little fishing expedition. For him it was a fairly delicate job.

"We just stopped by the house and saw the Murphys. They look pretty bad. It's tough being out of a job at their age."

Hobby's eyes flickered. He hesitated for a second. Then he said, "It's good to see you show concern for older people, Wally. Few of your generation do. I'm glad to say, however, that you needn't worry about the Murphys. I had a talk with them some time ago, and they agreed to stay on in the Canby house as caretakers after Mr. Canby was gone. Of course their salary will be small, but they have a nest egg, and will have no rent to pay, so they will manage quite well."

So there *was* an understanding between Hobby and the Murphys! They had something going, and they didn't want it messed up. But was it worth murdering for? Certainly not, from any rational standpoint — except that murderers aren't always rational. Remembering Hobby as he had been the night before, remembering how coldly furious he was, I was ready to keep all options open.

"Have you talked to them this morning, sir?" I asked.

"Yes, I phoned to see how they were."

"What did you think about Mr. Canby saying, 'Otis!' just before he died?"

"I don't know. It's not much to go on. It's a pity he didn't go into more detail," added Hobby with an unexpected flash of grim humor. He almost smiled. "One thing, at least, I won't have Mr. Fournier to contend with now."

"But maybe he'll claim his uncle wanted him to be curator."

Hobby's mouth hardened.

"Mr. Canby's verbally expressed wishes are one thing. Recording them with his lawyer in the cold light of day is another. If Otis Fournier tries to claim the position I shall resist with every — But I rather doubt that he will. I think he was only trying to please his uncle."

With that he turned and peered out his window at the Village green.

"Well, this is all very interesting, but in the meantime that pesky grass is continuing to grow, and I noticed on my way in that the flowerbed in the southeast corner could do with some weeding and edging. . . ."

A moment later we were on our way to work. As we walked toward the maintenance shed to fetch the tools of our trade Wally said, "Well? How about him and the Murphys? Is he being cagey? The business about the Murphys will have to come out,

38

anyway, so he lays it on the line right away to a couple of kids who can later testify he was perfectly open about it."

"I don't know, I just can't see him as a murderer."

"Neither can I — not shooting someone, or stabbing — or even poisoning someone himself, but I can see him telling someone else. . . . Besides, look at the situation. Here was an old guy who was on his way out, definitely on his way out. He was sick enough to die any minute. But if he lived one day longer he could really mess up the works for a lot of people. It was bound to be tempting It wouldn't be like knocking off somebody in the prime of life."

"Just a mercy killing, huh?"

"Well, the mercy would be for the survivors, not the victim," Wally admitted. "But anyway, it's a possibility. Meanwhile, let's have a look at the magic word!"

We had entered the maintenance shed, a long, low building where tools and equipment were kept and everything smelled either earthy or oily. A good smell. Nobody else was there. I pulled the crossword puzzle book out of my hip pocket, and was surprised when I read its title.

"*The Times Crosswords.* Say, these are English puzzles!"

"You were expecting French?"

"No, I mean English English."

Wally grabbed the book and riffled through it.

"Only about half of them have been done, so it's probably the one that — Here! Look at this!"

Under the diagram of a nearly-finished puzzle was a word printed in spidery block letters:

NAUSEA

"Nausea! Does that tell you anything, Les?"

"No. But let's see. . . . You remember what Mr. Canby said to Otis? Something about how this was the answer and now he should work out the clue? First we've got to figure out what he meant by that."

"First we've got to find out how these crazy puzzles work," said Wally, frowning over the book. "They don't look like regular ones at all."

I took the book and returned it to my hip pocket.

"Later. Right now, if Hobby doesn't see us working real soon, we'll be in trouble."

"Okay, okay. But . . . Nausea? . . . What could that mean? And what's it got to do with a list of old pictures?"

We didn't get to sit down and really learn something about those English crossword puzzles until after a lot of weeding and mowing, but finally the opportunity presented itself.

You know how the usual crosswords work. If the clue for a six-letter word is "Camera support," the answer is probably "tripod." If the clue for a two-letter word is "Egyptian sun god," the answer is "Ra." But these didn't work that way. They fooled around with words. They used puns and anagrams. It took us a while to get used to them.

The number of letters in each answer was given in parentheses after its clue. Of course, you could look at the diagram and count the number yourself, but sometimes the answer would be more than one word, in which case it would give you something like "(3,4)", or "(6,2)."

After we had read the introduction, which explained how the puzzles worked, we tried out clues from some of the earlier puzzles on each other.

"Get this, Les. 'Rested by sitting again for the artist.' Seven letters."

I gave up.

" 'Reposed.' See? It means 'posed again,' and it also means 'rested.' "

The clues had to be read in different ways. For instance, I tried this one on Wally.

" 'Was crazy when the bell sounded indeed.' "

He gave up.

" 'Deranged.' The bell sounded—rang. Put rang in 'deed' and you've got 'de-rang-ed,' which is 'crazy.' "

"It sure is!"

"So what would be a clue you could answer with 'nausea'?"

Wally sighed.

"I think this is going to take a little time."

I picked a clue out of a puzzle that hadn't been worked yet.

"How about this? 'Two inexpert ice skaters? They should be home by the fire!' Three words, four, two, eight."

We decided to put that one on the back burner and think about it, just for practice.

"Well, what about 'nausea,' now?" I asked. "It doesn't tell *me* anything, but the old man must have been trying to tell Otis *something*."

"We'll work on it."

"How about Uncle Matt?" I asked. "I suppose you're going to tell him all about this?"

"Oh, sure! Can't you see him? He'd raise the roof, and he'd confiscate the book! No, we'd better be quiet about it — unless we work out something that looks important."

"I just hope Kevin doesn't notice the book is missing and put two and two together."

"The desk was closed, wasn't it? You left it closed, didn't you? So why would he go looking in it for anything?"

"I hope you're right."

"Of course I'm right! When was I ever wrong?"

Wally wasn't half the worrier I was.

When Uncle Matt showed up that night, we had

just started to eat. He sat down at the table and sighed like a man with a weight off his mind.

"Well, Doc Hartley finally gave us his autopsy report. No signs of poison or anything like that, and plenty of evidence of a massive heart attack. So that's that."

Matt Brenner was an honest, conscientious police chief who loved his hometown. He didn't want a murder case involving prominent citizens; it would be bad for everyone. Wally, though, had definitely been hoping for a good murder case. He was disappointed, and his response had a needling quality to it.

"Case closed, huh, Uncle Matt?"

"There never was a 'case,'" snapped the Chief. "Well, at the beginning there was just an outside chance, of course. Naturally I made sure right away that Canby hadn't already changed his will. It would have been like him to have done that and not admitted it to Otis or Hobson, just to keep them wriggling. So I called Ernie Beemis."

Ernest Beemis was Mr. Canby's long-suffering lawyer.

"Of course, I had to hear a lot of guff about private information sacred to a lawyer and his client, but even though he's a lawyer Ernie Beemis has heard of justice, and in the interests of justice he finally came through.

43

" 'Well,' he said, 'Mr. Canby did phone me earlier on the day of his death to say he was going to see Otis and wanted to change his will — again — but of course he did not live to do it.'

"I thanked him, though not before I'd had to hear how he wished he had a nickel for every time he had been dragged over to change that will.

"Not long after I talked to Ernie, Otis came storming into the police station. He had realized I'd put a watch on him. When I told him I only wanted to make sure he stayed in town till the autopsy report had been made, he laid on the indignation with a shovel. There's nobody can act the part of an insulted pillar of society like the Otis Fourniers of this world. You'd think he'd never seen the inside of a police station before, whereas I happen to know he's been in and out of them from coast to coast. He could write a tourist guide about them. In fact, I even booked him once right here in Adamsport. Whole thing was smoothed over, of course, but there you are. He pulled himself up like a plaster saint and said, 'I'd hardly leave before my uncle's funeral,' and slammed the door behind him. I felt like saying, 'No, nor before the reading of the will, either.' "

"You think there'll be something in it for him, Uncle Matt?"

"Oh, sure."

"Not as much as he'd like, but something," agreed J.G.

Otis Canby had died on a Sunday night. The funeral was scheduled for Wednesday morning. On Tuesday afternoon Hobby summoned us to his office.

"I want you to take tomorrow morning off to attend the services. In view of Mr. Canby's generosity to the Village and your connection with him, you should of course be there."

Wally was pleased to hear this.

"You're absolutely right, sir — in fact, we would have asked for time off if you hadn't offered," he told Hobby, but he didn't add what he told me later — "Besides, I wouldn't miss the funeral for the world. I want to see how everybody acts!"

When we came home for supper that night Mrs. Brenner had a message for us.

"Mr. Beemis called. He wants you both to come to his office tomorrow afternoon at three o'clock for the reading of Mr. Canby's will."

"What? Why us?"

J.G. looked up from his newspaper.

"You must be beneficiaries. He's probably left you each a million bucks."

"Now, J.G., don't get the boys excited. He's probably left them some little keepsakes, or a small —"

"I'd hold out for a mill each if it was me," insisted J.G.

We were amazed, of course, and it was impossible not to get a little excited. After all, we had our normal share of greed.

"Who needs a million?" I said. "I'll settle for ten cents on the dollar."

"He liked us better than Victor," said Wally. "I wouldn't blame him if he left us his whole wad! Wouldn't blame him at all."

"Your mother was right," said J.G. "Don't get your hopes up. He probably left you his old garden tools."

"We'd better break the news to headquarters, Wally. This means we'll have to take the whole day off!"

"Call him. He's probably still at the office."

He was. But if we thought we were going to miss a whole day's work, we had another think coming. When I told him we had to be present at the reading, he said, "Very well. Then the time between the funeral and our appointment at Mr. Beemis's office will give us a good opportunity to get that inventory out of the way. Mr. Canby wished you to assist me with it, and I intend to respect his wishes," he said with an edge to his voice. "We can meet there at twelve-thirty."

When I repeated what Hobby had said, Wally

said, "Hey, why not?" and his eyes took on that scheming glint I knew so well.

During dinner there was considerable speculation as to the contents of the will.

"Victor will get all the big stuff," said J.G. "Otis missed the boat by one day. Even though the old man wasn't fond of Victor, there's no one else. But besides stocks and bonds and land, I'll be interested to see if any gold turns up. Old Canby was a gold bug, you know. He was talking gold at least twenty years ago, I know that for a fact. He came into my store one day and said, 'Gold, Mr. Brenner,' he said, 'put your money in gold and hold it.' I wish I'd listened to him. They say he bought gold coins——"

"Maybe when gold went so high he sold it, Pop."

"I doubt it, Wally. He was one of those that kept saying gold was going to over a thousand dollars an ounce. No, I'll bet he still had it, and I wonder what he did with it? I know he'd hate to see Uncle Sam get any of it — he hated the tax people. He hated taxes, period! Why do people who can most afford to pay them always hate them the worst? If he'd had, say, a favorite son, you can bet he'd have fixed it so his boy could get hold of his gold without having to report it. As it is, I suppose it'll turn up as part of the estate and Uncle Sam will have the last laugh."

"Good," grunted Uncle Matt. "Uncle Sam hasn't had much to laugh about lately."

At that point, of course, none of us knew whether there really was any gold, let alone anyone who knew where it was.

5

WHEN WE HAD A CHANCE TO talk I found out what Wally had in mind about the inventory we were going to do.

"What we need is a list of the pictures, and here's our chance to get it! While we help Hobby do the inventory we've got to make ourselves a list of them."

"Fine! But we're only doing an inventory of one room. What about Mr. Canby's room, and out in the hall — some of them are out there, I noticed. How do you expect to get a look at them and stand around making notes, with Hobby's eagle eye on us the whole time?"

The Wally Brenner look was in place.

"Don't worry, we'll manage. Hobby will probably give us each a clipboard. He's a clipboard man if I ever saw one. So every time he gives us the name of a picture to write down, we'll also put it on another list for ourselves. Don't worry! I'll work it out!"

It was the biggest funeral Adamsport had seen in twenty-five years.

The Canbys had been one of our first families since Colonial days, and old Otis was the last of the Canbys. And of course everybody in town knew how the cousins felt about each other, and that they would both be present at the funeral, so a lot of people were curious to see how they would act. Like Wally.

"Hey, Les, let's go early and get a good seat!"

"You make it sound like a ballgame," complained his mother. She looked us over and sighed. "It's a shame someone has to die to get you two into neckties and jackets!"

"We'll see you there, Mom. Don't be late!"

We hopped on our bikes and got there half an hour ahead of time. The church was already half full.

The Murphys were present, sitting well back in the middle of a pew, looking as if they didn't want to call attention to themselves. After we sat down Wally nudged me.

"Hobby."

He was four pews ahead of us on the other side.

50

Before long he craned his neck around for a general look and gave us a pleased nod.

Also present off to one side was Uncle Matt. It was natural he'd come to the funeral of a prominent citizen, but was he keeping a discreet eye on a few people as well? He might not want a murder case, but he was too conscientious a police officer to shut the door on the outside chance.

People filed in steadily. The Brenners joined Uncle Matt. J.G. saw us looking their way and winked, which got him a whispered scolding from Mrs. Brenner. She belonged to the school that didn't hold with winking at friends in church, especially not at a funeral.

The front pew on the right side of the aisle, customarily reserved for the family of the deceased, was empty.

"This ought to be pretty good," muttered Wally. "They'll have to sit together."

"Well, they can have a chat about the will while they wait."

Wally was quiet for a moment. Quiet, but not still. He couldn't sit down for more than two minutes anywhere without fidgeting. Under cover of the organ music we were getting, he whispered into my ear out of the corner of his mouth.

"Hey!"

"What?"

"I've got it!"

"Got what?"

"Those two inexpert skaters who ought to be home by the fire. Three words, four, two, and eight letters. Give up? Pair of slippers!"

I glared at him.

"You sure can pick a time!" I whispered. Actually I was only annoyed because I hadn't thought of it first. But nothing stopped Wally.

"How about that other one — 'perhaps let in a mad rush because he's so busy'? Seven letters."

"I'm working on it," I growled. We knew that "perhaps" usually meant an anagram was lurking somewhere. And a "mad" rush meant that "rush" was scrambled with something else that contained three letters.

The organ came to a quiet passage, so we shut up. A couple of minutes later the door to the sacristy opened in the front of the church alongside the altar and six men in dark suits filed out. The pallbearers. Victor led the procession. Otis brought up the rear, putting as many other pallbearers between them as possible.

Victor Ridgway was a big, burly, handsome man who was respected in the construction business as a man who knew every aspect of his trade.

"I can do anything I ask any of my men to do," he boasted, and it was true. He could work with his hands as well as anyone he hired. He also had brains and business savvy. He might have been well liked except for two things. He was often arrogant, and he was unquestionably the worst money-grabber in town. Even Otis Canby himself had seemed to find Victor's greed overdone.

"All the money in the world wouldn't satisfy Victor Ridgway!" was the way J.G. had put it the night before the funeral. "I'll bet he can't wait to get his paws on the old man's wad and the rest of the Canby land."

When Victor had married, his uncle had given him the plot of land Victor's house now stood on, about two hundred yards from the Canby house. Now Victor would probably own twenty acres more. The property line ran along the base of a low hill behind the houses on Salem Road. The land had not been farmed for sixty years or more, and was thickly wooded. All of us kids had grown up playing in those woods. Everybody along Salem Road was worried about what would happen now. J.G. had said a few words about that last night, too.

"You watch, he'll subdivide it and put in a whole new development. We'll have crackerbox houses in our backyards, with maybe twenty feet between them, unless the zoning board is on its toes! And you can bet there will be a new house slapped on the Canby house's foundations before his uncle's cold in the ground!"

Well, anyway, in they came. Victor's face was stiff and hard. Otis was trying to look solemn, but not altogether succeeding. His black mustache twitched like cat's whiskers once or twice, and his heavy eyelids drooped down like hoods to conceal what might well have been a wicked twinkle. Had he managed to get under Victor's skin in some way? Merely his being there was probably enough to do the trick, for that matter.

Victor led the group into the front pew, which creaked as it took their weight. The sacristy door opened again, and the black-robed minister appeared. The four ushers came down the aisle, two by two, and took seats in the left-hand front pew. The service began.

Stepping to the lectern, the minister intoned the opening prayers, then instructed us to stand and join in singing Hymn 115. I doubt it was a favorite hymn of the deceased, since he was not known as much of a churchgoer. In fact, I doubt it was anybody's favorite, being one of those Welsh dirges that can spoil a whole day; but at any rate, we struggled through it.

Next came more readings from the Scriptures, and then the minister launched into his eulogy. Most of his facts had already been in the newspapers.

Otis Canby had had one child, a daughter, who died in infancy. He was an officer in the Navy during World War I. After the war he became a stockbroker and for forty years, until his retirement, he was a partner in a firm in Boston. That had kept him in the city a good deal of the time, but like a loyal Adamsporter he had returned home for most weekends and summer vacations.

No reference was made to his grieving survivors, which was pretty smart under the circumstances. All in all the minister did pretty well. I'm sure he was glad when the job was over and the pallbearers brought the coffin up the aisle.

Otis was at the front on the left side, Victor on the right, and now it was Victor's turn to enjoy himself. He gripped his handle as easily as if he were carrying a light suitcase. He probably could have carried the coffin by himself. But for Otis, pudgy and out of condition, it was a different matter. His eyes bulged in their pouches, and his double chin quivered from the strain. Victor kept his gaze sternly ahead, but unquestionably he was watching out of the corner of his eye and savoring every moment of that long walk. It seemed to us he deliberately kept the pace as slow as possible.

If a nasty chuckle had come from inside the coffin as it went by, we wouldn't have been surprised.

The cemetery was not hard to reach. It was on the hill just behind the church. All the Canbys were buried there. It was the oldest cemetery in town, full of our Puritan forefathers and their descendants, so old it was quite a tourist attraction in itself.

Most of those who had attended the service showed up at the graveside, including Hobby and the Murphys. The customary words were said as the coffin was lowered into the ground — "ashes to ashes, dust to dust" — and Victor and Otis did their duty, each tossing symbolic handfuls of dirt into the grave, Victor first, then Otis. Neither so much as glanced at the other, and they found separate ways of leaving after the final prayer. As the rest of the crowd moved away, however, Wally lingered. He stood looking down into the rectangular pit at the coffin that now rested on the bottom. He brooded over it, a diehard to the end. I had a pretty good idea what he was thinking: that the body was there for future reference, if needed.

"Wally, you never give up, do you?"

His grin was half shamefaced, half defiant.

"Let's say I'm having grave doubts," he suggested

6

By THE TIME WE REPORTED to the Canby house, Wally had done some planning.

"Listen, you write faster than I do, so I'll write slow and make enough conversation to keep Hobby's attention away from you, and you write down the list."

"How come I always end up with the dirty work?" I complained, but of course I ended up agreeing.

Even though we got to the house at twelve-thirty sharp, we found Hobby already there, talking to the Murphys in the kitchen. He wasted no time leading the way upstairs after first handing us each — a clipboard. And a pencil, freshly sharpened.

"As long as Mr. Canby provided me with two assistants," he said in a dry voice, "I may as well let you give me a double check. I will dictate a brief description of each item in the room, and you will each write it down on your pad."

Hobby followed instructions to the letter. Not once did he so much as touch anything in the room, but he gave us careful descriptions of each piece of furniture, each rug, lamp, and piece of bric-a-brac.

When he came to the pictures, I wished I knew shorthand. The thing that saved me was the fact that he couldn't resist giving mini-lectures on some of them.

"Ah! Now here we have a well-known but fairly rare engraving, *Fishing Boats in the North Sea*, by Alexander Bishop, an American artist. Do you have that down?" he asked, and repeated it. "Bishop was a remarkable artist who unfortunately drowned at an early age, not at sea but — of all places — in Walden Pond! I trust you boys have heard of Walden Pond?" he said in the kind of voice people use when they trust you haven't.

I couldn't resist.

"We read the book," I said. In our part of New England they saw to it you did. Hobby blinked.

"Well! I'm glad to hear it," he declared, and passed on to the next picture. "And here is a treasure! *Harbour Scene, Alexandria, Egypt, 1871*, by Robert Forbush. Forbush's series of Mediterranean ports of that era is of the greatest importance "

That was the word we were looking for. Importance. I scribbled away for all I was worth.

Actually, the inventory didn't take long. When it was finished, and I was wondering how we were going to get a crack at all the other pictures, Wally said, "Mr. Hobson, we heard Mr. Canby say that some of the pictures in this house are important. Besides that one by Forbush, which ones do you think those would be?"

"The other marine paintings," he said promptly. "The family portraits are undistinguished, the work of itinerant artists who are either obscure or unknown. Of course, they have some value as likenesses, however crude. But half a dozen or more of the marine paintings and engravings are of real historical and artistic importance."

Wally looked positively scholarly as he consulted his clipboard .

"Let's see . . . *Fishing Boats in the North Sea* and *Harbour Scene, Alexandria* — that's two of them?"

"Yes, indeed!"

"What about the other ones? Could you show us which ones they are, sir? I've gotten kind of interested in sea pictures, and so has Les —"

"Good!" said Hobby. I didn't say anything, though I could have said this was news to me.

"So if you've got time to show us . . ."

"Certainly. They're all on this floor," said Hobby,

in his element now. "First of all, there are the two here in this room, and then — come along to Mr. Canby's room. . . ."

Wally turned to me.

"Write 'em down, Les," he suggested. "We'll never remember them otherwise."

"A good idea," said Hobby, quite pleased with us.

From then on, of course, it was a breeze.

Even with our extra guided tour the whole business didn't take long, so we had time to go back to Wally's and take a good look at our list of important pictures before we had to show up at Mr. Beemis's office.

This is what we had:

Mr. Canby's room

Grey Hunter, Capt. Abner Canby, Hong Kong Harbour, 1853, by a famous Chinese port artist.

The Battle of Lake Erie, 1813, from a contemporary painting. (A Canby was there with Perry.)

An early engraving of *U.S.S. Constitution* ("Old Ironsides").

Mrs. Canby's room

Fishing Boats in the North Sea, by Alexander Bishop, American artist.

Harbour Scene, Alexandria, Egypt, 1871, by Robert Forbush, big on Med. ports.

Hallway

Shearwater, Capt. Seleck Canby, Singapore Harbour, 1871, by Wang Hui-Ming, Chinese port artist.

Discovery, Capt. James Cook, Sandwich Islands, 1779.

We didn't have much time to work on the list before we had to leave, but offhand we couldn't see an obvious connection between any of the pictures and the magic word.

"Well, I didn't expect it to be easy," said Wally. "We'll work on it when we have time."

"Maybe there just *isn't* any connection."

"Maybe not. Maybe 'nausea' is a big nothing, for that matter — but at least we can give it a try. Maybe Hobby's idea of which pictures are important is different from Mr. Canby's — but somewhere in that house, and probably on the second floor, there's a picture that's important to Otis. I'd sure like to know which one!"

The neckties and jackets had a workout that day, because naturally we kept them on for the reading of the will. At ten to three we were climbing the stairs in the building where Ernest Beemis had his office on the second floor.

It was an old-fashioned building with high ceilings and wide corridors of varnished floorboards that creaked under every footstep — just the place for a successful and conservative Yankee lawyer.

The door said ERNEST K. BEEMIS, ATTORNEY AT LAW. It opened into a small reception room where a white-haired lady sitting behind a desk looked as if she had been sitting there for fifty years, which she probably had. She gave us a birdlike glance and picked up the phone.

"The boys are here, Mr. Beemis. . . . Yes, sir."

She motioned to the inner sanctum. We opened the door and learned that when it comes to the reading of a rich man's will the parties concerned tend to be more than punctual. Facing us behind a large desk was Lawyer Beemis. In front of him in a semicircle, twisting around for a look at us, sat Otis Fournier, Shapley Hobson, Kevin and Agnes Murphy, and Victor Ridgway.

It was interesting to see how they looked at us. Otis? Friendly interest. Hobby? Speculative, somewhat disapproving. The Murphys? Embarrassed, as though suspecting we'd be surprised to see them. Maybe it was just a carryover from the way they felt when the others saw them there. Victor? Suspicious, as though actually fearing we might have pulled off some kind of fast one with his uncle that would chop a chunk off his inheritance. In the past

Victor had largely ignored us. We had known him for three years, but we didn't really know him at all.

Mr. Beemis was a tall, thin, bald man who had been one of the pallbearers at the funeral. He'd had a pained expression then, as though he expected to suffer a hernia, and he had a similar one now as he peered at us over half-spectacles. In one form or another, a look of suffering was apparently his normal expression.

"Come in, boys. Take seats here, please."

He gestured toward two chairs placed beyond Otis on the left-hand side of the semicircle. We both mumbled something meant for general distribution and slipped into the chairs. Mr. Beemis consulted his wristwatch.

"Well. Since everyone is present, we may as well begin."

In the heavy silence that greeted this announcement the crackle of the sheaf of papers he picked up sounded like a forest fire.

" 'I, Otis Randolph Canby, make this my last will, hereby revoking all previous wills and codicils,' " Mr. Beemis began reading, and seemed to sigh slightly, as though remembering all those previous wills and codicils. " 'FIRST. I direct that there shall be paid from my estate my debts, the expenses of my funeral and of settling my estate (including the expenses of any ancillary administration) and any and all taxes on account of any property, including life insurance, included in my gross estate . . .' "

Mr. Beemis droned on, losing most of his audience for the time being, until some of the introductory stuff was out of the way. But then ears perked up again when he reached the first bequest.

" 'I bequeath the Canby family house standing at the corner of Salem Road and Old Farm Road in the town of Adamsport, Massachusetts, and the sum of Fifty Thousand Dollars ($50,000), to the Adamsport Village Association . . .' "

For the first time since we had arrived, somebody smiled. Hobby not only smiled, he positively beamed.

"Fifty thousand dollars as well! I must say, that is handsome. That will not only provide for the costs of moving the house but will leave a substantial sum for maintenance and repairs for many years to come!"

"I am sure we all share your happiness, Mr. Hobson," said Mr. Beemis, though Victor did not look particularly thrilled to hear that fifty big ones went with the house.

Before he went on to the next bequest, Mr. Beemis looked around our semicircle without glancing directly at Otis Fournier, and his pained expression was back again.

"You must all understand that some of what follows is Mr. Canby's own wording. I was not always successful in restricting him to customary legal phrasing."

He cleared his throat and read on.

" 'To my worthless rapscallion of a nephew, Otis Canby Fournier, I leave the income of a lifetime trust fund of Two Hundred Thousand Dollars ($200,000), which sum is to be disposed of upon his death as will be stipulated in a later clause. I further direct that the income from this fund is to be paid to Otis Canby Fournier only so long as he remains a legal resident of Adamsport and resides in Adamsport at least ten months of every year beginning with the next calendar year after my decease.' "

Mr. Beemis's glance topped his half-spectacles again.

"Somewhat unorthodox language, but —"

"Poor Uncle Otis. He didn't live quite long enough to change it," rumbled Otis Fournier, and chuckled wryly. Coming from an uncle worth several millions, the income from two hundred thousand dollars did not sound like much of an inheritance for even a worthless nephew, especially when it meant living in a small town ten months a year. But Otis did not seem downcast. Victor preserved his standard stone face, even though he was undoubtedly relieved to know that the sum wasted

65

temporarily on Otis was not larger. Was he thinking about what the difference might have been had their uncle lived another day?

The next bequest caused more of a flurry.

"In accordance with an agreement made between myself and Kevin and Agnes Murphy at the time I took them into my employment, I bequeath the income from a lifetime trust fund of Twenty Thousand Dollars ($20,000) per year for each year they remain with me . . .' "

Five years times twenty thousand made a very nice arrangement for the Murphys! Their patience in dealing with Mr. Canby became suddenly more understandable. Kevin's jowly cheeks were pink, and Agnes's pleasure was tempered by that embarrassed, defensive look we had seen before.

After an initial start of surprise, Otis leaned forward and beamed at the Murphys while Hobby offered his congratulations.

"I'm very happy for you both — and I hope this won't cause any change in your plans for the future," said Hobby.

"Oh, not at all, sir!" said Kevin. "We're very fortunate, to be sure, but . . ."

"Mr. Canby was more than generous with us," said Agnes in a sticky tone of voice that conveyed sainthood on the old rascal.

"Not at all!" said Otis. "You were a great help

and comfort to him, you deserve every penny you got!"

As for Victor, he actually managed a grim smile, and his comment went straight to the point.

"You earned it!"

Mr. Beemis cleared his throat. Silence reigned again. He now considered Wally and me with a glance that seemed to say, "What is the world coming to?"

" 'SEVENTH,' " he began, that being the clause he had reached, " 'I bequeath to Lester Cunningham and Wally Brenner a sum of money not to exceed Five Hundred Dollars ($500) each, to be used for the purchase of motorbikes.' "

We were knocked out. Old garden tools indeed! We felt like jumping up and getting off a few war whoops — but there was poor Hobby sitting there rolling up his eyes and suppressing a groan, so all we did was grin at each other like idiots and murmur something inadequate like, "Gee, thanks!"

"Don't thank me, it certainly was not my idea," said Mr. Beemis, but for the first time in our brief acquaintance I thought I saw something like a twinkle in his eyes.

Otis had not missed Hobby's reaction. He laughed heartily as he leaned sideways and slapped me on the knee.

"Good fellows! Now you can really bring this town to life!"

And now, finally, we came to Victor. We had provided a little comic relief, but now the main act was on. Everybody was quiet again. Victor sat with his hands folded in his lap, looking as if he were taking his own pulse.

" 'EIGHTH,' " read Mr. Beemis, " 'I bequeath to my nephew Victor Canby Ridgway the parcel of land described in the deed which . . .' "

A description followed of the twenty or more acres of land known locally as "the old Canby farm." Victor looked happy about that and waited for more. Once the old Canby farm had been disposed of, Mr. Beemis paused. He turned a page. When he resumed reading there was a tremor in his voice. Even Mr. Beemis was not immune to drama.

" 'NINTH. I direct that the balance of my estate be used to establish a nonprofit corporation to be known as the Canby Foundation, its purpose being to encourage and assist with financial aid those civic, cultural, and charitable organizations and projects which the board of directors of the Canby Foundation shall deem worthy of such encouragement and assistance . . .' "

A blockbuster. Here was good news for Adamsport but terrible news for Victor. If a face that was already a stone face can go blank, his did. Otis was less reserved. He let a high-pitched giggle get away from him for a split-second, then choked it off and spoke in a sanctimonious voice that must have been gall and wormwood to Victor.

"Splendid! How splendid of Uncle Otis! A tribute to the family, a lasting tribute! How much better than — than anything else he might have done with his fortune!"

Hobby said nothing, probably feeling it was wiser to spare Victor's feelings, but he did not look unhappy as he no doubt thought about possible pickings for the Village Association.

"The benefits to Adamsport are, of course, incalculable," said Lawyer Beemis in a dry voice. He read some further stuff about how the money from the lifetime trust funds would go to the Canby Foundation upon the decease of the beneficiaries, but nobody was paying much attention. Soon he was shuffling together his papers and saying, "My secretary will distribute copies of the will to each of you, and with that I believe our business is completed."

We walked downstairs with Hobby.

"Even from the grave," he mused, "even from the grave Mr. Canby managed to give me one last — last — what do you boys call it?"

"A zinger, sir?"

"A zinger. Yes, Lester, I suppose that will do. One last zinger. I am sure he must have read my letter in the newspaper. However, considering how worthwhile his other bequests were, one can forgive him. But if you bring those foul contraptions to work, you are to park them in the most distant corner of the employees' parking lot, is that clear?"

For once that night we were the ones with the inside information. When the will had been examined by one and all, and we had finished our account of events at Lawyer Beemis's office, Uncle Matt said, "Well, J.G., you win the clouded crystal ball award this time. Victor gets the land, all right, and of course that's worth at least half a million now and plenty more when he develops it — but that leaves a few million that got away."

J.G. admitted his mistake.

"I didn't take into account the fact that the old man was the last of the Canbys. Naturally he began to think about wanting to perpetuate the family name, and he couldn't do that by leaving his money to someone named Ridgway or Fournier. And since he wasn't charmed with Victor anyway, it was a good out."

Wally leaned back from the table and grinned.

"Well, I don't know about the others, but I'm satisfied. Motorbikes! How about that?"

His mother shook her head and moaned.

"One more thing to worry about!"

7

NO QUESTION ABOUT IT, THAT Friday was our busy day. After supper we took off for Wheels, Adamsport's only motorcycle shop. Wally had called Dinky Davis to tell him the news, and Dinky said, "Hey, Wheels stays open till eight tonight. I'll meet you there!"

Uncle Matt was going that way, so we decided to grab a ride with him and walk home, instead of taking our bikes. There was something about riding to a motorcycle shop on bicycles that bothered us, anyway, now that we were practically part of the motorcycle set.

Wheels was run by an energetic outgoing maniac named Ed Nagle. When we arrived he and Dinky were waiting for us. Ed shook hands and shouted,

"Congratulations, guys, I just heard the good news! You've come to the right place!"

Ed always spoke in a loud voice, even when he wasn't trying to talk over the sound of motorcycles.

"You've come at the right time, too," he added, "because I've just got in my first model of the hottest item going!"

His voice dropped to an almost reverent tone as he breathed the name.

"The new Yamakura!"

"I'm going to trade in for one as soon as I can!" said Dinky. "Wait'll you see it!"

We had a wait of about four seconds, which was the time it took Ed to march us across the showroom to a gleaming red number that took our breath away. It had everything going for it you could think of.

"I'll squeeze everything I can into your five-hundred-buck limit!" Ed promised.

"Well," I said, "of course we don't know just how soon we'll be getting our —"

"Who cares? Listen, it's like money in the bank, so I'll bet your folks would advance you three hundred apiece on the strength of it, and I'll wait for the rest!"

Before we got out of there, our Yamakuras were on order.

"Take about a week, maybe ten days, but I'll get right on 'em, don't you worry!"

We felt so good we all went to Gilhooley's for

Banana Bombshells, Gilhooley's improvement on banana splits, and sat around discussing strategies for arranging parental loans. What with one thing and another it was about ten when we started home. Before long we were passing the corner where the Canby house stood, well back from the street, deep among shade trees, with a few lights shining from the windows.

"Look at that," said Wally. "You know something? I'll miss the old place."

"I can't remember when it wasn't there," I said, and got a crack on the arm.

"I mean it, you twerp," he said. "I'll miss the woods, too. They were great to play in when we were growing up."

"They're not gone yet. We'll throw ourselves in front of the bulldozers."

"Forget it. They'll go. Good old Victor will develop every inch of that land. Bunch of new houses or even condos up there, with the trees gone and everything manicured."

"Cheer up. Maybe he'll put in a nice shopping mall instead."

"You just said that to make me feel good," growled Wally, but he stopped looking so gloomy. After a couple more blocks he was himself again. Far back in a side yard between two houses a small flickering glow caught his eye. He pointed to it.

73

"The Campfire Girls are toasting marshmallows. Let's scrounge a couple."

Linda and Marsha Gurney were twelve-year-old twins who had lived a few doors from Wally ever since they were born. In summer they pitched a tent out in back of their house and spent a lot of time there. They were good-natured, wide-eyed, scatterbrained girls of whom it had been said (by Wally) that because they were twins they had split one IQ between them.

Wally knew a marshmallow campfire when he saw one. The girls were holding toasting forks over the fire in front of their tent.

"Stick on two more, you got company," he said as we walked toward them. By the light of the campfire we could see four big eyes batting at us.

"Is that you, Wally?" squeaked Linda, or maybe Marsha.

"No, it's Count Dracula, and this is my assistant Jack the Nipper. We're calling for the local blood bank, would you care to contribute?"

"You scared us!" said Marsha, and now we could tell which was which, because their voices were a little different.

"We already had one scare, and that's enough," added Linda.

"Oh, did you, now? What kind of scare?"

"Well!" said Marsha importantly. "Wait till you hear!"

"I'm waiting."

"Well!" said Linda. "We had just come out here, hadn't started our fire or anything — in fact, we didn't start it till just a little while ago — but anyway, we had just come out —"

"When all of a sudden we heard this rustling in the woods!"

"Someone was coming!"

"On the trail!"

"We hadn't been talking or making a noise or anything —"

"That'll be the day," said Wally.

"No, really! We weren't speaking."

"We'd had a disagreement about TV. Marsha said —"

"Never mind!" Wally held up a stern hand. "It happens you were not speaking for three minutes, which is your outside limit, and weren't making any noise, so whoever was coming didn't know you were here."

"That's right. We were picking up twigs, and we weren't being noisy about it. Well, we looked at each other and dropped right down — but quietly! —"

"We scrunched down in the grass and watched the trail."

"In a minute this man came along. . . ."

"He wasn't making much noise, but he wasn't really sneaking along, either —"

"But nobody would have known he went by if we hadn't been out there."

"It was getting pretty dark, but he went by real close to us —"

"And he sure didn't look like anybody out for a walk in the woods. He was wearing a suit and carrying one of those cases like Daddy carries his papers in, only bigger."

Daddy was a lawyer. "You mean a dispatch case?" asked Wally.

"Yes, I think that's what he calls it."

"But you didn't recognize the man?"

"No."

"Did you go in and tell your family about him?"

"No."

"For Pete's sake, you dummies, why not? He could be a prowler looking for a house to rip off!"

"Well, I can give you a good reason why we didn't tell our family," snapped Linda. "Nobody's home!"

"You can say that again!" agreed Wally, tapping his forehead, but some of the wind was out of his sails. Marsha added her bit.

"You don't think we'd be here now if they were home, do you? We're not supposed to be out here at night!"

"Well . . ." Wally struggled to resume the attack. "But you could have run up to my house and

76

told my Uncle Matt! You know he's there a lot, and he's there tonight!"

"Oh, who'd think of that? You make it sound like — He wasn't sneaking along, he was just walking the trail, and he didn't even look at our house. And he certainly didn't look like any burglar! He didn't even have on burglar clothes!"

"Burglar clothes?" Wally snorted. "What's that?"

"Well, you know. Dark clothes."

"Okay, so maybe he wasn't a burglar. But are you sure it wasn't anyone you know?"

"Of course! If it had been we'd have said hello."

"So what size was he? Tall, short? Fat, thin? Old, young?"

"Well, not too tall, but sort of fat, or anyway pudgy —"

"And he had a mustache. I could see that much. He had a mustache."

That sent some high voltage through both of us. Wally's voice crackled.

"A mustache? A black one?"

"Well, it looked black in the dark, naturally! But I think it really was black anyway."

By now Wally and I were exchanging significant glances all over the place.

"The trail starts just a little ways from the Edgewood Motel," Wally reminded me, as if I needed reminding. "If somebody wanted to go from there to the Canby house without making a public spectacle of himself, and he knew the trail from living here off and on . . ."

"Maybe that's it, Wally," I agreed.

"So why don't we just hit the trail ourselves and see if we can get any idea of —"

"We'll come too!" said Linda.

"No! You've heard the expression, too many cooks spoil the broth?"

"No."

"Well, you've heard it now. And too many snoops spoil the snooping."

"We're coming," said Marsha.

"No!" Wally had to get rid of them. "Listen, we've got to split our forces. You want to do something important? Run up to my house and tell Uncle Matt all about this. Don't forget pudgy and black mustache. Tell him we've gone to the Canby house and if we find out anything interesting we'll be right back. By the way, how long ago did the guy go by?"

"Well, let's see . . ."

"It was right after *Slap Happy* —"

"We always watch *Slap Happy* —"

"That was what our disagreement was about. Marsha said —"

"Please! We haven't got all night. How long —"

"Well, *Slap Happy* goes off at nine —"

"Nine!" Wally glared at his wristwatch. "And it's almost ten-thirty!"

"You jerks!" I groaned. "He's probably come and gone by now, if it was him!"

"Was who?"

"Whoever it was."

"Well, he didn't come back this way," said Linda.

"Unless it was when we went in the house," said Marsha, which got her a hard look from her sister. "Well, we did go in the house for a while after he went by . . ."

"Yes, but we came out again, almost half an hour ago. . . ."

Wally rolled his eyes around hopelessly.

"Well, come on, Les, let's have a look anyway."

"Do we still have to go tell your uncle?" asked Marsha.

"Yes! And be sure to tell him you saw the guy an hour and a half ago, so he'll know that if it was a burglar instead of — of someone else — he's probably cleaned out a house and gone across the state line by now!"

"He carried away a whole houseful of stuff in his little dispatch case, I suppose!" said Linda. Those twins were not really as dumb as Wally liked to pretend. Just young.

"Well . ." For want of something better, he issued an order. "Go on, get moving! And don't forget — pudgy, and black mus——"

"We know, we kno-o-o-w!"

8

I T WAS A DARK NIGHT, BUT WE
had both known the trail all our lives. As we hurried
toward the Canby house we felt frustrated.

"We've probably missed the boat! We'll be lucky
if we find out a thing!"

"Well, there's a chance he's still there — if he
went there."

"Where else would he be going, Les? The big
thing is to make sure it was Otis the twins saw and
not somebody else."

"Burglars make a lot of money these days, they
can afford to dress well, but has it got so they carry
dispatch cases to work? I thought they made do
with pillowcases."

"Right. That wasn't any burglar the twins saw.
But how come Otis would be calling on the Mur-

phys? Tell you what — why don't we just knock on the door and ask Kevin if Otis Fournier is there?"

"And if he says yes, then what?"

"Wait! I've got a better idea! How about telling him the truth? Tell him the whole story and say we wanted to make sure it was Otis and not a prowler?"

"Hey! Now you're talking! Why, we'll even get brownie points for that!"

The path curved around the back of the Canby house and ended (or began, depending on which way you were going) at Old Farm Road, the street that ran up past Victor's place. We cut through the woods, came out into the yard, saw lights in the house, and headed for the back door. We were nearly there when the outside light popped on. The door opened and someone we had not expected to see came rushing out. Victor Ridgway, breathing hard.

"Hey, boys! Did you see anyone come this way just now?"

"No!"

"He went out the front, but he might have doubled back around the house. . . ." Victor was really nerved up, wild-eyed and sweating. "I almost caught up with him, only while I was coming in the back he left by the front!"

"Well, we didn't see anyone — but the Gurney twins saw a man coming this way on the trail."

"What? When?"

Wally quickly explained, and described the man. The effect on Victor was spectacular.

"Thank you, Wally! Thank you!" He bared his teeth in a frightening smile that suddenly reminded me of his late uncle, and said, "I didn't see him myself — but now it all adds up! Come in here! Come in!"

We hurried inside with our ears flapping. Victor's big rugged face was not only working, it was working overtime. He looked mad and exultant all at once.

Wally said, "We sent the twins to my house to tell Uncle Matt," and that set him off again.

"He's there? Good!" Victor grabbed the kitchen wall phone receiver and thrust it at Wally. "Tell him to come down here!"

While Wally dialed, Victor paced the kitchen floor.

"It adds up. It all adds up. But — what time did you say those girls saw this man?"

"A little after nine."

"But that's crazy! What the devil was he doing here for an hour and a half?"

Wally hung up.

"Uncle Matt's already on his way."

"Okay! Now I want you to tell him what you told me, and then I want action!"

Victor was on his way out of the kitchen to the

front hall, with us right on his heels. We could hear tires crunching gravel out front. Victor opened the door and ordered the Chief to hurry. Uncle Matt came in at his own pace.

"Matt, I want Otis picked up as fast as you can do it, because he's just robbed this house!" barked Victor as soon as he'd shut the door.

"Do you know for sure it was him, Victor?"

"The boys here —"

"The Gurney kids told me all about it, but there's a lot of men around with black mustaches."

"Okay — but you'll change your tune when you've heard my side of the story. Shortly before nine I got a call from Agnes Murphy. She said Otis had just phoned and asked them to meet him at the Peabody Inn's coffee shop in Balmoral. He said he had something confidential to discuss with them that would be greatly to their advantage as well as his. He said it would be better if they got together some-place where local people wouldn't be likely to see them."

"I wouldn't pick the Peabody Inn for that," said Uncle Matt. Balmoral's about a thirty-minute drive from Adamsport, but the Peabody Inn is a well-known and popular place.

"Neither would I, but then who ever said Otis was bright? Anyway, they told him they'd come. But then they got to thinking about it and decided to call me to see if I thought they should go. They're in the habit of depending on me for a lot of things, which is something my fool of a cousin didn't know, I suppose.

"I told them, sure, go ahead and see what he has in mind, but don't commit yourselves to anything, and let me know what he's got up his sleeve. And with that I didn't stop to think much more about it, because I was expecting an important call from out of town and wanted to get Agnes off the phone.

"I'd hardly hung up when I got the call, and for the next hour I was on the phone most of the time. It was only when I had a chance to catch my breath and sit down with a drink that I began to think about Otis and the Murphys again. And then the thing hit me that I should have suspected right away — that maybe Otis was just getting them out of the house. Maybe he wanted a clear field so he could go in and grab something, maybe something Uncle Otis told him about that last night, or something he spotted. It was just the kind of sneaky thing he'd do!

"The first thing I did was call the Peabody Inn to see if Otis had really met them there. I described the Murphys and asked the clerk to see if they were in the coffee shop, and if they were alone to ask one of them to come to the phone, but not to bother them if anyone was with them.

"Pretty soon Agnes got on the phone. Otis hadn't turned up. I told her to stay there for another half hour or so, just in case he still showed, and then come home. I hung up and came straight down here to check the place, and that's it. I was really surprised, because I figured if Otis had been up to something he'd have come and gone a long time ago. Instead, I heard someone upstairs. Now, I didn't get a look at him, so I can't say for sure it was Otis, but if that isn't enough circumstantial evidence —"

Uncle Matt was already on his way to the phone.

"It'll do for now. I'll get the State Police on it as well as our own men. He has a rented car. I have the license number here in my notebook. We'll start with the motel, though it's my bet the car will be there and he won't."

Victor took Uncle Matt to the kitchen phone, Uncle Matt made his calls, and then Victor said, "Now let's go upstairs. When I came in I heard sounds up there, as I said, and like a fool I went right upstairs, but by that time he'd gone down the front stairs and out the door. If only I'd gone straight through the house!"

As Victor led the way, the picture of him charging up the back stairs while Otis raced down the front ones gave me some low entertainment.

We entered Mr. Canby's bedroom. The rolltop desk was a worse mess than ever now. The top had been rolled up, and papers were tumbled around and strewn on the floor. The bed was neatly made up, but a large framed engraving was lying on the

86

quilted bedspread. In the center of the space the picture had covered was a small wall safe. Its door was almost but not quite closed. Victor swept a ham hand that way.

"There you are! He was up here, and he must have been cleaning out that safe when he heard me come in!"

"You haven't touched anything?"

"Certainly not!"

"Good. Maybe we can lift some fingerprints."

"I tried to look inside the safe without touching it, but I couldn't see anything."

Uncle Matt took out a pencil and eased the door open with it.

"Yup. Nothing to see. Empty. Any idea what was in it?"

"I didn't know my uncle had a safe in here. He didn't take me into his confidence much. But I have the same suspicion everyone else is going to have."

"What's that?"

"Gold. I'm sure he collected gold for a long time. Coins, maybe even bullion. Maybe he showed some of it to Otis the other night. If he did, Otis would have had to help him get up and go over to the safe — either that, or open it for him."

Uncle Matt gave the safe a close inspection, glanced around the room, and went to the phone that stood on a bedside table, looking out of place in such a setting.

"I've got a man who's good with fingerprints. I'll get him over here."

While he was making his call I sidled toward the bed and nearly bumped into Wally doing the same thing. We were both trying to get a good look at the picture.

It was one of those sentimental jobs that were very big in Victorian times. It showed a faithful shepherd dog mourning beside his master's grave. This wasn't hard to figure out, because it was titled *Shepherd Dog at His Master's Grave.*

And it wasn't one of the pictures on our list of the valuable ones.

Uncle Matt finished his call, then stood pulling reflectively at his lower lip as he studied the safe again.

"Why would he take an hour and a half to open that thing?"

"That's what beats me," said Victor. "If he knew the combination he should have been in and out of here in ten minutes, and no one the wiser — in fact, he could still have met the Murphys and handed them some cock-and-bull story."

"Maybe your uncle hadn't given him the combination yet, so he had to look for it," said Uncle Matt, eyeing the desk. "People always have a thing like that written down somewhere."

Victor was eyeing the desk too.

"Or maybe he was looking for something else. I wonder what his story will be? He's got some explaining to do, but knowing him—"

"He may deny everything."

"He'll probably try to," agreed Victor. He hauled in a big breath and let it out hard. "Well, why should I worry? It's no skin off my nose — anything he took belongs to the Village now, anyway. It's just that — well, it would really burn me up if that louse got away with this! But wait a minute — how can he deny it all? How can he deny he called the Murphys and then didn't show up?"

"He can claim he didn't make the call."

Victor thought this over.

"My God, he could, at that. He could claim the burglar imitated his voice, to get them out of the house!"

The phone rang. Uncle Matt answered, grunted a few comments, and hung up.

"He hasn't been picked up yet. And his car's still at the motel."

The doorbell rang.

"Probably Greg Newton. Les, go down and let him in."

Greg Newton was the fingerprint man. He checked the safe and was disappointed.

"Wiped clean."

Uncle Matt pointed to the picture on the bed.

"Try that."

Greg did, and brightened.

"Some beauties here!"

"Good. Wipes the safe, but gets scared off before he remembers the picture. Lift them, go dig Otis Fournier's set out of the files, and compare them. Call me here."

"You've got his prints?" asked Victor, then answered his own question. "Oh! That business, years ago? . . ."

Uncle Matt nodded in an absent way as he watched Greg go to work. When Greg had left, he began a thorough inspection of the room. There was not much he missed on the tables, on the walls, on the floor, even under the bed, and one thing he didn't miss made him start pawing through his pockets.

"Let's see, where's my — ? Here we are." He brought out a pair of tweezers. "Handy things to carry. Surprising how often I find a use for them."

Kneeling down and grunting forward over his paunch, he reached under the bed and brought forth a bright round disc. A gold coin.

"Careless. Dropped one." He glanced up at Victor. "Looks like you might be right about what was in that safe."

Victor stared, and his face twisted into a hideous grin.

"Shapley's not going to like this. He's not going to like this at all." The grin faded as he glared at the coin. "That fat sneak! I wonder how much he got away with?"

Uncle Matt was still poking around examining everything when the phone rang again. He answered, said thanks, and hung up.

"The prints check. Now all we need is Otis."

9

VICTOR WAS OLD STONE FACE
again.

"Good. At least now we know," was all he said.

From downstairs came sounds of the back door
opening and closing. Kevin called up the stairs in
a worried voice.

"Mr. Ridgway?"

"Come up!"

The Murphys hurried upstairs and came into the
room.

"Oh!" Agnes Murphy's eyes went straight to
the safe.

"You knew about the safe?" Uncle Matt asked
quickly.

She looked scared, but said, "Yes, sir. One time
when I was dusting the picture frames I decided

they could use a wipe-off with an oil rag, the wood was awful dry, so I was taking down a picture off its hook when Mr. Canby came in — he was still able to get around then — and he asked what I was doing. When I told him, he said all right, to go ahead. Then he pointed to that picture, the one on the bed there, and said I'd find a wall safe behind it. He said he only used it for a few personal things, so if we had anything we'd like him to put in it for safekeeping, he'd do it."

"And did you give him anything to put in it?"

"Oh, no, sir! What if we'd given him something and then something happened to him and nobody knew the combination —"

"Or . . ." Kevin nodded heavily in the direction of the looted safe. "Not that we have many valuables to worry about, but . . ."

"I guess we should have mentioned the safe to Mr. Beemis — or to you, Mr. Victor," said Agnes in a worried tone. "But that was long ago, when we first came here, and I don't think it's crossed my mind since."

"Mr. Fournier never showed up at the inn, did he?" asked Victor.

"No, sir, he didn't," said Agnes, and then she gasped. She stared at Victor, and at Uncle Matt. "You mean, Mr. Fournier . . . ?"

"He just wanted to get you out of the house," said Victor.

To forestall more questions Uncle Matt gave the Murphys a brief account of what had happened. When he reached the part about the safe he said, "There's no telling what he took out of it, but there was probably some cash as well as the gold. . . ."

"Gold?" cried Agnes, and it was just as well for her she did, because the Chief wasn't missing a thing. ("Just testing," he told us later. If the Murphys had heard him say gold without reacting, he might have thought they knew more about the contents of the safe than they were letting on.)

But Agnes's eyes were out on sticks, and so were Kevin's.

"Yes, there may have been some gold in the safe," said Uncle Matt. "However, we'll keep that point to ourselves for the time being, because we're not really sure." He finished his briefing quickly, and then said, "Now, I think we may as well call it a night and get some sleep, and maybe by morning Mr. Fournier will turn up and we'll have a chance to hear his side of the story."

Victor gave his prediction.

"He won't admit a thing. I'll bet he'll even give you some sort of malarkey about the fingerprints. Know what he'll say? He'll say Uncle Otis asked him to straighten that picture the night he was here! You wait and see, he'll come up with something!"

Agnes balked at that.

94

"Well, he won't get away with it! I cleaned every inch of this room after . . ." But then she faltered. "Come to think of it, though, I only dusted the furniture and the pictures with a feather duster. . . ."

"See what I mean?" said Victor.

Uncle Matt gave us a ride home and came in with us. Moments later we were all sitting around the table having coffee and he was saying, "I'll be surprised if Otis gets picked up very soon. By now he must know every way there is to slip out of a town. Or he may have friends here we don't know about, someplace where he can hole up till the heat's off. Of course, he might be lucky if he was picked up, because right now I don't see how we can charge him with much more than trespassing, and that's not much of a charge — and maybe no charge at all against a nephew who can probably produce a set of keys to the house and claim his uncle gave them to him."

"Now, wait a minute!" protested J.G. "He opened that safe, didn't he?"

"It looks like he opened the safe. But that's not the point. Tomorrow morning I'll check with Ernie, but I'll bet he doesn't even know there's a wall safe in Canby's room, let alone what was in it. In other words, except for Fournier, the only person who could tell us what was in that safe is dead. So what's to keep Otis from saying his uncle gave him the combination, and what's to keep him from saying he opened it and found it empty? We can think anything we want to, but we can't prove one blessed thing was in it. Even that coin I found doesn't really prove anything."

"You don't really think he found the safe empty?"

"No. I think there was gold in it, and maybe some other stuff, and my hunch is the old man wanted Otis to have it, and would have set things up for him if he'd lived another day. I think you were right, J.G. — Canby wanted to pass his gold along without letting the tax people know about it. Maybe he told Otis there was a safe, but hadn't given him the combination yet. Maybe he was thinking about giving it to him the next day. Naturally it never occurred to him he might die suddenly. We all think we're going to live forever, even when we have one foot in the grave. He thought he'd be able to take care of everything in the morning."

J.G. turned his attention to us.

"Well, you two seem to have some prize experiences in that house."

Wally glanced at me and said, "We sure do, Pop." We were feeling guilty twinges about recent experiences we'd had there that we'd kept to ourselves. I looked at my watch.

"Guess I'd better go home and check the house. How about riding over, Wally?"

"Okay."

We took off on our bikes and had a talk as we went.

"I notice you didn't say anything about the Yamakuras, Wally."

"Of course not. Gotta pick the right moment, when there's not so much competition for their attention."

"Yeah, but the sooner you get an okay, the better. Makes it that much easier for me."

We waited till we got to my house to talk about the thing that was really on our minds. We sat down on the lawn out in back.

"Well, what about that crossword book?" I said. "We're withholding evidence from Uncle Matt, aren't we? What are we going to do about it?"

"Nothing. Maybe it doesn't mean anything. If we tell him about it now we'll just get in trouble for nothing. Whatever it meant to Otis, it's pretty plain he's already made use of it."

"Well, yes. But . . . 'Nausea'! If you can tell me what that could have to do with a picture about a faithful shepherd dog, I'd like to hear it."

"I don't think it has anything to do with Otis's knowing where the safe was. Probably his uncle told him where it was, but didn't give him the combina-

97

tion, like Uncle Matt says. 'Nausea' must have had something to do with something else."

"I don't know, I'm beginning to wonder. Maybe we *are* making too much out of it. Maybe it was just for fun."

But Wally shook his head.

"I can't sell myself on that idea. Otis was too anxious to get his hands on the book and work on that word. It meant something important to him."

"It did look that way."

"Anyhow, I'm not going to give up yet. I'd like to figure out the crazy thing just for my own satisfaction. But I can tell you one thing — I'm not going to stick my foot in a hornet's nest by telling Uncle Matt about that book when probably nothing will come out of it anyway. If we ever think of something that makes sense and gives us a lead, then we'll have to tell him and take our lumps."

"Okay with me. I'm not looking for trouble. Why, a thing like that could wreck our chances of getting our bike loans!" Then I had a sudden happy thought. "Matter of fact, though, I guess we can stop worrying. Now that the stuff in the desk is all messed up, Kevin's not going to notice the book's missing and put two and two together."

"There is that. Yeah, that helps," said Wally, and got off a typical Wally Brennerism, accompanied by a sly grin. "Yes, sir, that's a big relief. I don't have half the trouble with a guilty conscience when I'm not worried about getting caught!"

"You've got a great criminal mind," I said

"Thank you."

I had to take him down a notch.

"By the way, talking about those crosswords, remember the one we figured must be an anagram? 'Perhaps let in a mad rush because he's so busy'? Seven letters? I've got it. You put 'rush' and 'let' together, mix 'em up good, and get 'hustler.' See? A guy who's 'so busy.' "

Wally didn't even change expression.

"Good, Cunningham. Very good. You may go to the head of the class. Somehow that reminds me of the one about 'How Mrs. Sprat would talk to Jack at mealtime.' Three words — four, three, and three? Come, come, Cunningham, surely you remember your nursery rhymes? 'Jack Sprat could eat no fat, his wife could eat no lean'? So how would Mrs. Sprat talk at mealtimes? 'Chew the fat,' of course!"

So much for bringing him down a notch.

10

OTIS WAS STILL AT LARGE next morning. The bare bones of the story had to be released. No mention of gold, of course, and all the reporters were able to report about Otis was that "Mr. Fournier was being sought for questioning."

"Well, I hope he found a fortune in that safe, because he's blown his nest egg," said J.G. "If he comes back to Adamsport he'll be arrested, and if he doesn't he won't qualify for his trust fund. Of course, if he really found a pot of gold he may be willing to pass up the fund."

"I don't think he was anxious to live here ten months of the year," said Uncle Matt. "An island in the Caribbean would be more his style."

Sunday night my folks got home from their trip. I had a lot to tell them, needless to say, including the big news about the motorbikes. Once I got to that, and had described the reading of the will, I brought up the deal Ed Nagle had offered us.

"Wally's folks went for it, but that doesn't mean you have to," I said with total insincerity. "I can wait. It's just that . . . well . . ."

My father gave me a hard look.

"Nothing doing."

Then he said, "I just wanted to see the look on your face if you had to wait. Okay, it's a deal — but with certain restrictions! . . ."

They were the same restrictions Wally's folks had laid down, practically to the letter, but we'd already decided we could live with them.

A week passed. Nobody had yet been able to lay hands on Otis. And in the meantime, we had other things to think about. We kept in close touch with Ed Nagle, who assured us everything was going according to plan. To keep us happy, he let us practice riding on a couple of old bikes he had around, so that we'd be ready to take off when ours were delivered.

Meanwhile, Hobby was already arranging for house-movings, because Ernie Beemis was clearing the way for him to go ahead. Naturally Hobby wanted the house as soon as he could get it, in time for the summer season when the tourists gave us our biggest business. First the Tavern would have to be taken to a new location, so that the Canby house could be moved to its original site. Victor Ridgway was a help to Hobby there, because he'd had dealings with house-moving outfits and knew whom to get.

We had expected to pack up all the exhibits and furnishings in the Tavern, maybe even empty the building before it could be moved, but the contractor said that wasn't necessary. Mr. Caselli was an expert and proud of it.

"You can leave everything in place. If you leave a pencil on the table we won't roll it off."

The plan was to move the Canby house a week or so after the Tavern. Thanks to Hobby's and Victor's persistence, a date was set for the Tavern that was three weeks to the day after the funeral and the reading of the will.

In the meantime we kept fooling around with those cryptic crosswords. Neither of us liked to give up on a puzzle of any kind, and neither one of us could really believe "Nausea" didn't have some special and important significance as far as Otis was concerned. So we learned more about the puzzles.

For instance, we found there could be hidden words in the clues.

"Get this one, Les. 'Is Igor ill again? Not entirely, the big ape!' A hidden word!"

"What?"

"Look for it, you big ape!"

After a minute I found it — "gorilla" — and later I found a hidden word in the clue, "Stop in this abode, sister."

"Stop" was the definition word. Stop! Desist! Sometimes one word was inside another.

"How about this one?" I had the pleasure of saying one night. "And in Dad there's an animal.' Another name for 'Dad' is 'Pa.' Now put 'and' in 'Pa,' and what have you got?"

"P — a . . . Panda!"

We were getting pretty good at solving the puzzles, but we still couldn't put "Nausea" together with the faithful shepherd dog — or with any of our list of supposedly important pictures, for that matter. Any way we twisted them around, the only thing "Nausea" suggested was seasickness, and that didn't seem to tell us anything.

Our motorbikes were finally scheduled for delivery on a Monday, which suited us fine because that was our day off. We waited for Ed Nagle's call, then pedaled over to his shop like a couple of Italian bicycle riders. This time we rode our bikes because they provided the fastest way of getting there.

The sky was looking nasty again.

"I suppose it'll pick today to lay another thunderstorm on us, just when we want to ride around," I grumbled.

"Naw, it'll hold off," said Wally, who was always a determined optimist when pessimism became unbearable.

When we showed up Ed was yakking with another man. He looked around and said, "Here's the kids I was telling you about. Well, guys, there's your wheels."

The Yamakuras were ready and waiting. The next few minutes were pure bliss as we admired them.

"Must have been a pretty nice old geezer, to leave them the dough for these," said the other man.

"Well, not everybody thought he was so nice, but he did treat the help pretty well," said Ed. "He left the couple who took care of him the income from twenty gees a year for every year they'd worked for him, and they were with him five years."

"No kidding! You know, that sounds familiar. Where did I —? Yeah, I remember. When old Miss Frost died over in Bromwich she left money to the people that took care of her. It was the same sort of deal."

Not many things could have taken our minds off our new bikes at that moment, but the mention of Bromwich did it. I looked around at the stranger.

"Are you from Bromwich, mister?"

"Used to be. I live in Boston now."

"When were you in Bromwich?"

"Most of my life. My family still sends me clippings from the local paper now and then, that's how I happened to read about old Frostie. Why?"

"I just wondered if you remembered the name of the people who were left the money. . . ."

"Hmm . . . sorry, no. I didn't pay that much attention to the story — I'd been away for a while, and —"

"The people here were Kevin and Agnes Murphy," said Wally. "That ring any bell?"

"Murphy. I knew some Murphys in Bromwich, but they raised chickens. I went to school with one of the Murphy kids — Jimmy Murphy, he was —"

"But you didn't know Kevin and Agnes, huh?"

"No, afraid not. And I don't know who the folks were that worked for old Miss Frost, but they did all right. I think they'd been with her three or four years, and she left them the income from so much a year, I forget how much, for every year they'd been with her. She left a lot of other money, too — she was loaded."

The man from Bromwich had spoiled our concentration. We thanked Ed for making delivery. We said good-bye to them both, and asked Ed to keep our bicycles around till we could pick them up. We wheeled our Yamakuras outside and had the thrill of taking off on them. That kept us going for several blocks before Wally motioned me to slow down. We pulled over, stopped, and looked at each other.

"Remember that nephew of theirs who came by, Les?"

"Of course I do! I even remember his name."

"Danny."

"Right. Smart-aleck guy they didn't look too pleased to see. We figured he was probably trying to borrow money."

"And then when he left, remember what he said? 'So long, Uncle Kevin, I hope you do as well here as you did in Bromwich!'"

We were trimming bushes nearby at the time, couldn't help hearing, and couldn't help seeing how Kevin acted, either.

"Boy, did that make Kevin burn!" I said, and Wally did the mimicry.

"'That's in very poor taste, Danny. Now be on your way, and don't come back!'"

He followed that by recalling a more recent conversation.

"Hobby said they had a nest egg! You know — when we talked to him in his office, the morning after Mr. Canby died."

"Sure! He said they had a nest egg, and wouldn't have any rent to pay, so they'd make out okay!"

"Right! And where did that nest egg come from?"

Wally gunned his motor a couple of times. Never mind what Hobby thought, it was a lovely sound.

"It's a shame our folks had to make all those conditions. All those rules."

"They wanted a lot for their three hundred bucks!"

Condition Number One: do not ride your motorbikes outside of town until you have spent a couple of weeks learning how to ride them.

"Of course, they were talking about normal situations," said Wally. "This is not a normal situation."

"Sure isn't!"

"How far is it over to Bromwich? Can't be more than an hour, hour and a quarter. . . ."

"I think we're onto something," I agreed, casting caution to the winds. "Let's see, now — how do we get there?"

11

WE WENT BY KOLSKY'S GAS
station, where we could at least look at a road map.

It wasn't much more than forty miles to Bromwich, even by way of the back roads we decided we'd
better take. Most Adamsporters who were going
anywhere outside of town used the highways, so we
didn't want to be seen on any of those. Besides, the
back-roads route looked easy. Just a few twists and
turns, nothing special, not even for a couple of new
riders on new Yamakuras.

"It's a piece of cake, Les. Let's go!"

"What are we waiting for?" Wally wasn't the
only one who could swagger. But then as we put on
our brand-new helmets I squirmed a little. "I hope
Uncle Matt never finds out about this, though. You

know what he thinks about amateur detectives. He doesn't even like them on TV."

"Especially not on TV. But if we come up with something important, that'll be different."

"Okay. So when we get to Bromwich, what do we do?"

"Well, first we're going to find out where Miss Frost lived. If she was able to scatter money around in her will, that shouldn't be hard to do; she was a prominent person. Then we find the house and see what kind of stores and shops are in the neighborhood. Somebody's bound to have known the Murphys."

"If it was the Murphys."

"It *has* to be the Murphys."

"It better be," I said grimly. "Let's go find out."

We got in some good practice on the way to Bromwich, and only lost our way twice. Once there, we located the public library. If you want to find out where someone lives, or used to live, that's a good place to go. We told the librarian we knew some people who used to work for Miss Frost, and said we wanted to see her house, which was certainly true. The librarian was young, so even though she knew Miss Frost had been prominent in Bromwich she didn't remember anything about her. But she was able to look up the address we wanted and tell us how to get there.

All the time she was helping us, groups of two or three people kept showing up and trooping past the desk, chattering about books. When we were ready to leave, I said, "You're getting quite a crowd today."

"Yes, it's a regional meeting of the New England Library Association."

We were instantly on guard.

"Does that take in Adamsport?"

"Oh, yes. In fact, Mrs. Cranshaw from Adamsport is vice-president of our group. She'll be here, I'm sure. Are you from Adamsport?"

"Er — near there," said Wally, as we gave each other what must have been a very shifty-eyed glance. We had a sudden and overpowering urge to get out of there. "Well, thanks a lot for your help — come on, Les, we'd better get moving!"

We left the poor librarian with her mouth open and scuttled away. Not only did Mrs. Cranshaw know us well, she was a good friend of my mother, who was a volunteer helper at the Adamsport Library. As we came outside, a roll of thunder greeted us.

"All we need. Rain any minute. Did you say it was going to hold off?" I asked bitterly.

"Let's hope so," said Wally, not so sure now. "Let's just get away from here before —"

A car pulled up in front of the library and a woman got out. Who else?

"I won't be long. Get us some good seats," said the driver.

"I will," said Mrs. Cranshaw, and turned around face to face with us. She beamed. "Why, Lester! And Wally! What are you doing here?"

She pointed at the two Yamakuras parked where they probably shouldn't have been.

"Are those your new motorbikes? Why, I was just saying to Grace Hammerstein, 'I'll bet those lucky boys will get themselves something like those!'"

"That's right, Mrs. Cranshaw. You guessed it," said Wally with a sickly smile.

"We were fooling around, practicing on back roads, and got turned around," I said by way of making my contribution. "We didn't expect to wind up here."

"Well, I don't wonder!" said Mrs. Cranshaw. "Why, Bromwich is a good forty miles from Adamsport! You'd better get yourselves some road maps! But anyway — nice to see you, boys, and do be careful on those things!"

Mrs. Cranshaw hurried inside. We groaned our way down the steps.

"Now we've had it! We're dead. Unless we can go home with some spectacular information, we've really had it!"

It's not easy to bite your fingernails while riding a motorbike, but we almost managed the trick on our way to Miss Frost's house. It turned out to be a Victorian mansion in an old part of town.

"Kevin and Agnes must have used some of the stores and shops around here," said Wally. "Look, there's a little restaurant. Maybe they ate there sometimes."

"Maybe so. There's a cleaner's! If there's anyone who knows everything that's going on in the neighborhood, it'll be him. What do you say?"

The shop's sign read, *G. Levine, Cleaner*. A short, bald-headed man chewing on a cigar was working at a pressing machine, surrounded by racks of clothing.

"Good morning," said Wally. "Mr. Levine?"

The man pointed in the direction of the door and spoke around the sides of his cigar.

"Like the sign says."

"We were just looking at that house over there. Is that where Miss Frost lived?"

"Um."

"Did you know her?"

"Forty-five years in the neighborhood, did I know Miss Frost? — sure I knew her! Why?"

"Well, we have some friends that worked for her once, about five years ago —"

"The Murphys?"

The lightning that was causing more thunder outside might as well have passed down our spines.

Pay dirt, the first place we tried! You'd have thought Wally's voice was changing a few years late as he replied, "That's ri-i — that's right! Kevin and Agnes."

"There was a lucky pair!" said Mr. Levine, letting up on his pressing machine and pulling the cigar out of his mouth. "You know what they got out of her?"

"Some money, didn't they?"

"*Some* money? The income for life from eighty thousand dollars, that's what!" cried Mr. Levine, and told us all about the provisions of her will. We were elated. We stopped worrying about trivial matters such as meeting Mrs. Cranshaw, and waited as patiently as we could — waited to ask the all-important questions. When Mr. Levine finally finished, Wally asked one of them.

"How did Miss Frost die?"

Mr. Levine looked surprised.

"You don't know?"

"No. They never said."

"That's funny, because she died in a real crazy way, for an old lady." Mr. Levine was enjoying himself now, enjoying the chance to retell an old story. "She drowned in a bathtub!"

He relished our obvious astonishment. Certainly he never had a better audience. We were both too excited to speak. We were getting close to something. We *had* to be getting close to something. Wally finally managed to ask the next important question.

"In a bathtub! Gee, that is crazy! . . . Were the Murphys with her — er — I mean, they were working for her when that happened, were they?"

"Sure, they were working for her then."

"And she was an invalid, wasn't she?"

"Miss Frost? Not her! She was on the go all the time. She was on a trip to the West Coast when it happened."

"And the Murphys were with her?"

"Naw! She didn't need them on trips. They were here, taking care of the house."

A loud sound seemed to shake the floor of the shop. It was a thunderclap, but that was not what 't sounded like to me. To me, it sounded like two fathers and Uncle Matt all coming down on us at once.

It was three hours before we made it home. We got lost four times, and soaked to the skin twice, even though we did our best to travel between cloudbursts.

There was a council of war, and when it was over we were grounded. Our new Yamakuras were given a week's vacation. And then, that evening, Uncle Matt took us apart all over again.

"Didn't you think I'd already checked out the

Murphys?" he demanded to know. "*Naturally* they felt funny, and looked it sometimes, too. They hit the jackpot twice, and would just as lief not have the subject come up. It was lucky for them these reporters and TV newshawks today are too dumb or lazy to think of checking them out.

"They told me all about it. At the time Miss Frost died, their trust fund only brought in about six or seven thousand a year, but they could count on it. So they decided to ask their next employer for the same kind of arrangement, in return for which they accepted smaller salaries than they'd otherwise have asked for. It was a setup that suited Canby just fine, because he liked saving money while he was alive. At any rate, it's pretty plain the Murphys are not a pair of conniving murderers, so they ought to be left alone, and not have a couple of squirts prying into their lives!"

By this time we both had hangdog looks you couldn't have hung on any respectable dog.

"I've just turned in my badge," said Wally.

"Me, too," said I.

Uncle Matt gave us a glower apiece.

"Good! Let's keep it that way!"

12

THE NEXT MORNING WHEN WE
came to work we were told Hobby wanted to see us.
Our guilty consciences made us wonder if somehow
he had gotten wind of our day-off doings, but that
wasn't it.

"Mr. Ridgway phoned yesterday to say that the
cellar at the Canby house must be cleared out so that
Mr. Caselli's men can start work. He's going to
meet me there this morning with a pickup truck to
bring anything I want over here. There's a fine old
workbench and tools and a number of other things.
I'll want you to come along to fetch and carry. We'll
go over at ten o'clock."

We left his office and walked to the maintenance
shed.

"Funny how your mind works," I remarked. "Right in the middle of being depressed this morning about the mess we got into, I thought of the answer to that one about 'Silver in a circle makes one angry.' "

"Yeah?" Wally tried to show some interest, but didn't get far with it.

"Yeah. Good old Krumhoff's chemistry course gave me a boost. Remember that Table of Elements he was always stuffing down our throats? 'Ag' is the symbol for silver, and for some reason it's always stuck in my mind. So a circle is a ring, and if you put silver in it you've got 'raging.' "

Wally sighed.

"Pretty good. Now if you can think of an answer to 'confiscation of motorbikes,' we'll be all set."

When we arrived at the Canby house with Hobby, Victor was there with his pickup truck backed in close to the cellar doors. The Murphys had come out to ask if their help was needed. Hobby took the opportunity to tell them the Village would put them up at the Edgewood Motel while the house was being got ready to move. They looked worried, but said that would be fine. Needless to say, we felt funny when we saw them and thought about what we'd been up to the day before, but of course no one there knew about that, and nobody was paying any attention to us, anyway. Victor told the Murphys he wouldn't need them, and they went back into the house.

Victor opened the slanting doors and the four of us thumped down the wooden steps into the cellar, where we listened to Hobby rhapsodize over the workbench and tools.

"A veritable museum of Early American tools!" he said. Certainly it looked as if no Canby had ever got rid of a tool since Cap'n Seleck moved the house there, or before. They were hung on pegboards in meticulous order, and were well cared for.

"I don't think Uncle Otis ever used them, or knew how to, for that matter," said Victor, "but he liked to take care of them."

"He certainly must have!" Hobby touched one of them lovingly, and wiped his finger on a rag. "They all seem to have a good protective coat of oil on them."

Victor snorted.

"Had to, down here! Always damp. I don't mean to take anything away from Cap'n Seleck, he was a good shipmaster, but he was a poor judge of where to put a house. My hill behind here is full of springs, and about every other year for twenty years I've had to come down and get the sump pump going for Uncle Otis. Look at this! This house has sat here for over a hundred years and it still has a duckboard floor, because you can't concrete it! I tell you,

118

I wouldn't put another house on this site if you paid me!"

This last statement not only amazed us all but made us uneasy. If not a house, then what? A gas station?

"Well, I'm surprised to hear that, Victor," said Hobby.

"I'm sure you are, and so will everyone else in this town be. Nobody ever gives me credit for any feelings, but I *am* a Canby, at least on my mother's side, and I've decided to turn this piece of land into a park in memory of the family."

Hobby all but gasped.

"Why, Victor, that's handsome of you!" he said when he'd caught his breath. "That's very handsome of you!"

"We'll fill this in, landscape the whole corner, put in a little playground for the kids, and I'll take down the barn — it's not worth moving," Victor went on a bit glumly, as if he had suddenly realized how much money all this could run into, but knew it was too late to turn back now. And I might as well add that when Victor announced his plan a few days later there were cynics like J.G. who said, "Sure — a nice little park to class up the development he's planning!"

The Tavern was ready to be moved. The building was freed up all around the foundation, hot-air ducts leading upstairs from the furnace were cut, as were water lines and electric wiring. Adjustable steel posts became temporary replacements for uprights supporting bearing beams. The building was then jacked up on all sides. The jacks had steel rod handles six or seven feet long and were operated by hand, but under the building hydraulic jacks were also used. The Tavern was raised high enough for long steel I-beams to be slipped under the stress points. A three-point undercarriage of rubber-tired wheels, four pairs of double wheels to each set, two sets near the rear corners and one set centered forward, were attached to the rig, and the building was ready to be towed away by a truck.

It took Mr. Caselli's crew less than a week to get the Tavern ready to move. Hobby saw to it that moving day got plenty of advance publicity, which brought our turnstiles lots of business that day. And as soon as the Tavern was out of the way, some of the crew started pointing up the foundation, putting it in shape for the Canby house, and the rest of the crew began moving equipment over there.

By then we'd done our time as nonmotorbikers and were using them again — but not to go to work. Both our fathers were big on exercise for other people, especially us. I never noticed either of them getting a whole lot of it themselves, except for an occasional round of golf. Nevertheless, one of their conditions was that we would continue to ride our bicycles to work. When Hobby got wind of this he went out of his way to congratulate us on having such sensible parents. What a drag!

The evening before the Caselli crew started work at the Canby house we stopped by on the way home for a look at the grounds we had taken care of for so long.

"Well, Victor's park will never look as good as our place," said Wally, kidding and yet not kidding, if you know what I mean.

"Absolutely not." I glanced at the barn that Victor had said wasn't worth moving. It had been used as a garage by Mr. Canby when he was still able to drive, and by the Murphys since then. "I suppose Victor's right about the barn, but it seems a shame just to tear it down."

"Want to buy it and move it?"

"No. Say, I wonder if Kevin remembered to take the house key?"

There had always been a house key hung on a nail behind a beam just inside the door. I walked over to check. It was still there. I put it in my pocket.

"I'll give this to Kevin next time we see him." The Murphys had already moved to the motel.

I often wonder how things would have worked out if I hadn't taken that key.

***

All during that next week, while Mr. Caselli's men were gradually raising the Canby house from its foundations, we went by regularly to see how things were coming along. One night when we were riding around we saw a car with a man sitting in it parked in front. We turned into Old Farm Road and rode by for a look. We went on up the hill past Victor's place, then stopped.

"Wow! Did you see him, Wally? I didn't know King Kong could drive!"

"What's he doing there, I wonder? Pretty rough-looking customer."

"Not the friendly type," I agreed. "And big! Listen, maybe we ought to tell Victor about him."

"Why not? Could be he's casing the joint. We don't need any more break-ins. Hobby wouldn't like it!"

We went back to Victor's and rang his bell. After a minute or two he came to the door.

"Evening, Mr. Ridgway. We just went by the house and saw a guy sitting out in front in a car. We thought we ought to tell you, just in case."

Victor nodded.

"You're right. I'm glad you keep your eyes open. But he's okay — I put him there. What with all the publicity the house has been getting, I was worried for fear someone might try to break in, now that the Murphys aren't in the place. Mr. Hobson agreed, so I offered to pay for a watchman until the house is moved. He's Tom Bogan, one of my men."

"He looks like he can handle the job, all right," said Wally, and brought a hard grin to Victor's face.

"I don't think anybody will fool around with Bogan," he agreed.

"Well, then it's okay. Sorry we bothered you."

"That's all right."

We said goodnight and left. When we'd ridden away and were puttering along side by side, I said, "Well, he picked the right guy."

"I wouldn't want to wrestle him best two out of three."

By then we had pretty much lost interest in trying to make any sense out of Mr. Canby's magic word. Whatever it was, Otis had already gotten his mileage out of it. But we'd gotten hooked on the puzzles. They became a real test of one-upmanship, with each of us trying to outdo the other.

We were over in my kitchen having a late snack and testing our puzzle wits the night before the house was to be moved. Mom and Dad were playing bridge at some friends' house.

" 'Can people in them write rings around everybody else?' Two words, eight and seven letters. Don't tell me you haven't got that one yet?" I said.

" 'Literary circles'!"

"You're hot stuff with anything that has 'rings' in it."

"Yes, indeed. 'Silver in a circle makes one violent,' " I said, recalling my earlier triumph. "Raging.' "

"Wait a minute. Maybe that will help with this one. 'Strange tape around copper provides beverage holder.' What's the symbol for copper? Co? C-something, anyway."

"I'll get my dictionary. It has the Table of Elements in it."

Of course I took a peek at the Table on my way back. "Strange tape around copper" — that meant "tape" got mixed up around copper, which was "cu." I had the word and a smug expression both ready by the time I reached the kitchen.

"I should have remembered. Nothing to it. An easy one," I said, handing Wally the dictionary. As he looked at it I added, "As you can see, copper is 'cu.' Mix up 'tape' around it, and you've got your beverage holder."

Wally was staring hard at the table. I gave him ten seconds, then hit him with the answer.

"Teacup."

He wasn't even listening. He looked up at me with his eyes popping.

"Why didn't we think of that?" he said. "Gold is 'au'!"

He grabbed a pencil and wrote in the margin:

Then he put parentheses around "au":

N (AU) S E A

"N" often stands for "North" in cryptic puzzles.
I let out a yell.

"Gold in the North Sea!"

"Gold *hidden* in the North Sea! We've got it!"

"*Fishing Boats in the North Sea!* Something's
behind that picture!"

"Yes, but what? More gold? Another safe?
What?" Wally had jumped to his feet. "We've got
to find out. This could be real important!"

"Should we tell Hobby, or —"

"No! We can't be certain there's anything to it,
even now, and we sure don't want to tell anyone
about this puzzle book and explain how we got it
unless we have to! So first we find out for ourselves!
Now . . ." He stabbed a finger at me. "You've got
a key!"

"What? You mean —"

"Tonight's our chance to be in there alone.
There's no telling when we'll get another chance."

I laughed.

"Oh, sure — with that big ape watching the
place, we're going to sneak in and —"

"Right! Don't worry about him."

"How can I look at him and not worry about
him?"

"Aw, now listen, he's big, but I'll bet he's as

dumb as he is big. He probably sleeps in his car most of the time, maybe walks around the house every hour or so. We'll wait till he makes the rounds and gets back in the car, and then . . . We can't miss. Got some flashlights? Grab a couple, and let's go!"

13

As usual, i couldn't resist
this typical Wally Brenner plan. It was harebrained,
it was dangerous, it was crazy — and yet it wasn't.
We *should* be able to get in the house without Bogan
knowing it, if we waited till he was sitting out front
in his car. It was the best chance we'd have in a long
time of being alone in there long enough to find out
what *Fishing Boats in the North Sea* was hiding.

Besides, who could just sit around and wait with
a secret like that on his mind? We had to know. We
had to find out whether or not we had solved the
riddle of Mr. Canby's magic word.

"But listen, Wally, let's not go off half-cocked,
let's really think things through first. For instance,
clothes —"

"Right! You've got to get out of that white shirt

and those slacks and put on the darkest stuff you can find, and I've got to do the same."

"You can't wear any of my clothes, so what'll your folks think when you come in and change to dark clothes at ten o'clock at night? In summertime?"

"I'll drop them out of my window and change in the garage."

So a few minutes later we had parked the Yamas in Wally's driveway and he had gone inside and I was out in back under his window. His window screen slid up and a wad of clothes came down on my head. I took them to the garage. Wally wasn't far behind me.

"No problems?"

"No problems."

"Uncle Matt there?"

Wally nodded.

"They're playing pinochle, and Mom's watching television. I said hi, I wanted to get something, and that was it. They hardly looked up."

Wally put on dark slacks and a long-sleeved navy blue shirt and hid his other clothes in a corner of the garage.

"Got your flashlight?"

"Sure."

"And the key?"

"Yes."

"Let's go."

We slipped through the woods behind the house and took off along the trail. We had walked the trail hundreds of times at night, but it had never been like this. Never before had we tried to walk it without making a sound. Never before had we worried for fear someone just might happen to be out in his backyard at the wrong moment. We didn't want *anybody* to see us that night. Just the business of our dark clothes might be enough to start someone wondering.

Though the moon was not full, there was still more moonlight than we would have ordered if we'd had a choice. Wally stopped.

"When we get near the Gurneys' house let's make sure the twins aren't out in back."

"They can't be. They got in enough trouble for being outside that last time."

"That was weeks ago. They could be at it again by now. Anyway, let's be careful. All we'd need is those two in our hair!" said Wally, and the very thought sent a shudder through me. "What are you dressed like that for? Where are you going?" — I could just hear the questions they'd ask. We crept forward on noiseless feet.

We didn't need to bother. Nobody could have heard us, anyway. Lights were on all over the Gurneys' house, and out in the side yard girlish cries of glee filled the air. Sitting around a bonfire toasting marshmallows were the twins and about fifteen of their best friends. Well, actually, four or five. They just seemed like fifteen. Obviously the twins had special permission to have a party out there, and they were doing it up. We stopped cold, backed off a little way, and held a whispered consultation.

"Not a chance, huh? Ha!"

"I can't believe it!" I wanted to groan, but couldn't risk it. "Now what do we do? Cut back through the woods and go around them?"

"Are you kidding? You know how thick those woods are. We'd sound like a couple of moose trying to get through them at night! Listen, we've got plenty of time, so . . . we'll just sit down and be patient."

"What? You patient? This I gotta see!"

"Well, you're going to. The party can't go on forever. It can't be a pajama party, with the whole gang sleeping out here — there isn't room in the tent. So we'll wait 'em out, even if it takes —"

"Half an hour?"

This time Wally almost groaned.

"Not *that* long, I hope!"

So we sat down, and the marshmallow madness went on. And on. And on. And along with it came some dialogue we could have done without. The girls got on the subject of our big night. Somebody asked, "How did they happen to come here, anyway?"

Linda's laugh trilled through the night air. Her

voice, when she spoke, was like a claw running down our spines. "Oh, those silly boys! They wanted to mooch some marshmallows."

"It's pathetic," said Marsha in a similar voice. "And then, when we happened to mention the man we saw, Wally got all excited —"

"You'd have thought he was Cruncher Cristo," said Linda, mentioning a real jerk of a detective on a terrible TV crime show, "only he's not that smooth!"

"And Les! He stood there with his face hanging out and saying dumb things like 'He's probably come and gone now, if it was him!' and when I said, 'Was who?' he said, 'Whoever it was.' You know the way he talks!"

If my voice ever sounded like Marsha's imitation I'd join the Trappist monks and never say another word. I spent a long, long half-hour and more writhing at the things they said about me and grinning at the things they said about Wally, and he did the same in reverse. I was ready to write a severe letter to the newspapers about parents who let their twelve-year-old daughters stay out until the wee hours of the night, but finally the call came from the house for the party to break up, and after what seemed like another half-hour of dragging their feet they finally put out their fire, gathered up all their paraphernalia, and trooped inside.

***

"Oh, well," said Wally. "It doesn't matter. The later we get there, the more bored and sleepier Bogan ought to be."

"Bogan! He looks like something that should sleep in a tree."

"The car will do, if only he'll sleep. Well, the coast is clear here. Let's get moving."

"Those twins. We've got to think of something that's so rotten they'll never get over it. Maybe burn down their tent."

We slipped past the Gurneys' house and had no further problems the rest of the way. But when we reached the point from which we could follow a little side trail to the Canby house's backyard, we looked out at a patch of no-man's-land that the moon lit up like a spotlight.

"We've got to know where Bogan is," whispered Wally. "Let's go on to where we can see if his car's out in front."

We found a place where we could see the street. The car was there, and Something was in it that looked hulking enough to be Bogan. Wally was disappointed.

"I was hoping he'd be walking around, so that when he went back to his car he'd settle down for a while."

"He probably did that while we were pinned down by the twins!"

Wally sighed heavily.

"I guess this is our night for waiting. We've got to wait till he makes a move, and then we'll know better when to make ours."

"There's no other way," I agreed. "We might as well sit down right here."

So we sat down and waited. And waited.

That wasn't the best evening I ever spent, but it had to be the worst of Wally's life. Inactivity was real torture for him, and now after that session the twins had treated us to, Bogan was putting us through the wringer again.

"Maybe he's asleep."

"Maybe he's dead."

"No such luck," growled Wally under his breath. "I'm sure I saw him stir a little a minute ago. Listen, I've got an idea. Let's make our move now. I'll stay at the corner of the house to keep an eye on Bogan while you climb up and get the back door open — you can climb up easier. If he starts to get out of the car I'll give you the high sign and we can both hide before he gets anywhere near. Chances are he won't budge."

Even I was at the point where anything sounded better than just sitting around on the damp ground. The idea scared me, but it had its attractions, too. We got up and took a good look at the yard, the car, and the dark hulk in the front seat. The house looked forlorn sitting up in the air on I-beams, spending its last night at the old stand. Moonlight shone on the trees and bushes and on the ruts trucks had left in the lawn.

"Have that key ready."

"Don't you worry!"

It still looked like no-man's-land, all that open space between us and the house. I thought of those World War I movies where the men in the trenches went over the top. I knew how they felt now. Bogan couldn't have seen us from where he was, but even so it was creepy. We crossed the yard as fast as we could and still be quiet about it. Wally edged along the back of the house to the corner and checked the car. He turned and gave me the go-ahead signal.

I climbed up the crisscross of rough timbers that supported the I-beams, missing a heartbeat every time my foot scraped on the splintery wood. The back door wasn't exactly an easy entryway anymore. I had to balance myself alongside it while I tried to unlock it. And I had just taken the key out of my pocket when —

"*Psst!* Get down! He's coming!"

Wally gave me such a start I almost came down the hard way. And I dropped the key.

As I scrambled down Wally grabbed my arm and dragged me toward the cellar steps. The doors were gone. We shot down the wooden steps and flattened

134

ourselves in a corner where the workbench had been, just seconds before footsteps rustling in the grass told us that Bogan had come around the corner of the house. By now I was making up for those beats I'd missed, and I was sure my heart sounded like a bongo drum.

The footsteps stopped. We could hear Bogan humming something that sounded like *Mac the Knife*. Even his humming sounded tough. What was he doing? Was he thinking of coming down into the cellar for a look around?

A flashlight beam suddenly blasted the darkness. The beam made a tour of the cellar, as much of it as it could reach from outside, then snapped off. After a few seconds, it went on again outside, and I began to feel a little faint. What if he spotted the key I'd dropped? He definitely seemed to be sweeping his light around out there. If the key was lying on the grass, he could hardly miss it. . . .

It seemed forever before Bogan finally turned his flashlight off again. Still humming his sinister tune, he walked away. In a moment total silence made it seem pretty certain he'd gone on around the house, but we still waited awhile longer. Or should I say it took us a while to get up nerve enough to move. Then Wally nudged me.

"Okay. Let's go."

I gulped.

"Wally."

"What?"

"I dropped the key."

"*What?*"

"I dropped —"

"I heard you!"

"I think it went straight down. I don't think it hit anything. I hope it didn't bounce around!"

"Oh boy. Well, come on, let's look for it. I'll check on Bogan, and you look for it. You'll have to use your flashlight, but for Pete's sake be careful! Keep your hand over the light. Don't let any more show than you have to."

We crept up the cellar steps and, after a cautious look in both directions, got busy. Wally returned to his post at the corner of the house and signaled that Bogan was back in his car. As soon as he did I got down on my knees, turned on my flashlight with my hand covering the top, then let enough light through to show me the ground under the back door.

I'm a strong believer in the theory that Things have it in for us. I've noticed they pull every dirty trick they can. Drop a quarter on the floor, and it will hide back of a chair leg every time, or go down a hole nobody knew was there. So I was depressed before I even started pawing through the grass looking for that key. And my pessimism seemed justified. Not a gleam of metal showed up anywhere I looked. I glanced at Wally, a small, dim figure in the pale moonlight, and he gave me a hurry-up signal. I could well imagine the kind of pins-and-needles he was suffering.

There was nothing to do but keep looking. And just when I was ready to give up I caught a glimpse of something jammed as far under the edge of a clod of dirt as it could get.

The key. I grabbed it and signaled to Wally, who was glancing my way every few seconds. He raised a fist in the air, took a last look around the corner, and joined me.

This time I didn't drop the key.

14

THE HOUSE HAD BEEN SHUT UP for a week. Even though some of the windows on the north side had been left open a crack, the air was stale and stifling. We stood still for a moment, listening, and heard nothing. No car door opening or any other sound came from outside. The windowshades were drawn most of the way, but enough moonlight seeped in to keep the house from being pitch dark. Across the kitchen I could see the shadowy outlines of the table and chair where Kevin had sat reading his newspaper.

"I can see okay, can you?"

"Good enough."

The back stairs were something else, though — an upward-slanting black hole. And the treads seemed determined to creak and snap with every step we took. I don't suppose they were really very loud, but to us they were like firecrackers on the Fourth of July. We stopped halfway up and listened again, but again all seemed quiet outside. I wiped sweat from my face with my sleeve and took some deep breaths. We started on again, and finally reached the second-floor hall.

Mr. Canby's was the front room in the south-west corner. Mrs. Canby's room was also on the front side.

"We'll have to be real quiet —"

"And stay away from the windows!"

We tiptoed down the hall to Mrs. Canby's room. The doorknob squeaked as Wally twisted it and pushed the door open. We stepped inside. The window curtains were drawn here, too, but one window had been left up a few inches, probably an oversight on the Murphys' part, since rain might come in from that direction.

"Look at that! Wouldn't they forget that one?"

Wally looked on the bright side.

"He won't hear us if we're careful — but we'll hear him if he gets out of the car."

We crossed the room to the wall where *Fishing Boats in the North Sea* was hanging. Wally started to touch it, then pulled his hands back. As he reached in his pocket he said, "Give me your hand-kerchief."

With a handkerchief in each hand he took hold of the picture and eased it off its hook.

Even in the darkness we could see that the wallpaper outlined a small dark square. I stepped around Wally and took out my flashlight.

"Hold the picture up between me and the windows."

While Wally shielded me with the picture I let a tiny bit of light shine on the wall.

Set into it was a metal box with a keyhole in it. Like a safe deposit box.

We stared at each other and at the box as a lot of things fell into place. Wally jerked his head toward the door. I snapped off the light. He laid the picture on the bed. We tiptoed out of the room into the hall. When I had carefully closed the door behind us, we talked it all over in whispers.

"So that's it! The key!"

"Sure! The key to Otis's happiness. This is where Mr. Canby kept his gold, Les! He let it be known he had a wall safe, when all the time —"

"That's why he wouldn't let anything be touched or moved in here. He wasn't just being sentimental!"

"So Otis had the key, and figured out what his uncle meant by 'nausea,' and came up here . . and . . ."

No. No. It didn't work. The same thought bothered both of us.

"But he had the key! He could have opened the box, grabbed the gold, and been out of here in ten minutes flat!"

"Right. So maybe Mr. Canby put a clue in this box that made Otis go looking for something else. One of his puzzles."

"Well, maybe. But I doubt it. I think the gold was right here, and the minute he got his hands on it Otis would have taken off."

"So do I."

Then Wally's eyes seemed to flash in the dark.

"Okay, so let's try another angle. Let's say Victor was lying! Let's say he didn't come here after ten o'clock, he came right away. He caught Otis here and scared him off not long after the twins saw him on the trail."

"Around nine?"

"It's a possibility."

Everything was suddenly turned upside down, all the ideas we'd had. It took some getting used to.

Wally eased the door open. I followed him back into the room.

"Help me hang this." Wally lifted the picture. "Get the wire over the hook."

Together we replaced the picture. He handed me my handkerchief, and we both mopped our faces. I went to a corner of the window, checked the car, and nodded to Wally. We returned to the hall.

"Okay, Wally. Let's say Otis got here a little

after nine, came upstairs, and opened this box. He hears Victor coming, and takes off. Then why was the safe open?"

"Maybe he had time to empty this box and put the picture back in place and go take a look in the safe, too, before Victor showed up."

"Well, maybe. But then what did Victor do for the next hour and a half? Did Otis have to leave without the gold, did Victor find it, did he hide it somewhere? What did he do?"

"Well . . . Maybe it was Victor who opened the safe! It's a pretty sure thing he didn't know about this box, so he probably thought it was the safe Otis was planning to rob when he scared him off. Maybe it was Victor who spent his time looking for the combination."

A lot of maybes, none of which seemed to add up.

"Only one thing seems sure to me now. Victor was lying," muttered Wally. "And that means everything he's said about anything has to be taken with a grain of salt. For instance, those calls to the Murphys at the Peabody Inn. He probably made both of them from here."

"Yeah. And putting somebody here to guard the house — why should he worry about it so much when it's not his property? He's not the kind of guy to spend money when he doesn't have to, not even on a family house. So what's he really worried about?"

"Good question. And his big plans for this property. Why is he doing the Good Guy act with land this valuable? Does he really care about the family that much? Why make it a park? . . ."

Suddenly we knew.

Just like that, we both knew. There was only one answer, and it hit us right in the pit of our stomachs. We didn't stop to work out all the possible details, we hardly exchanged a dozen words about it, we just knew. Besides, we were instantly anxious to get out of that house. We both went to the window and took another cautious look outside.

"He's okay. Come on, let's —"

But as we watched, a car turned into Old Farm Road and pulled up alongside Bogan's. A big car, with Victor in it. Bogan, who had been slumped down in his seat, sort of sprang to attention in a sitting position, but that wasn't good enough for Victor. He jumped out of his car and tore into Bogan.

"I'm not paying you to sleep, I want you to keep your eyes open, and if you can't do that you won't have this job or any other, you understand?"

"Yeah, boss, I'm sorry!" Bogan crawled out of his car and all but cringed. "It's the night air. . . ."

After a while Victor simmered down, and by that time Bogan was thoroughly awake.

"Well, this is the last night, and I don't want to take any chances," Victor was saying presently in a more reasonable tone. "I don't want someone fooling around here and getting hurt. Tell you what. I'll come back in a few minutes and spell you for a couple of hours."

"Gee, that would be great, boss!"

"Okay. But let's have a look first."

We watched them start off around the house.

"Wow," said Wally. "The minute Victor leaves, if Bogan goes back to his car, we've got to get out of here!"

"Can't be too soon for me. But until they come back let's stay right here and keep quiet!"

Waiting again. They could have walked around every house on Salem Road while we waited. What were they doing? Had Victor noticed something? What was there to notice?

"I'm going to check from over there."

"Be careful!"

Wally went into the room across the hall. In a moment he returned.

"They're standing in the backyard, talking. Come on! While we've got the chance let's go down the front way and watch from downstairs. We'll be that much closer to the kitchen."

Anything that moved us nearer to freedom sounded good. We walked to the head of the stairs and started down.

We'll never know what was on those front stairs, but something made Wally's foot slip. He almost tumbled down them. He caught himself on the railing, but by then it sounded as if a herd of buffalo had been let loose in the house. From the backyard came a hoarse yell from Bogan.

"Hey! What was that?"

"Someone's in the house!" said Victor. "That came from the front. Come on, let's go around there!"

Wally recovered himself quickly.

"Here's our chance!"

We raced down the hall to the kitchen as quietly as we could, pulled open the door, and jumped out one after the other into the waiting arms of Bogan, who took pleasure in cracking our heads together.

"Got 'em, boss!" Bogan was one happy fella. His efforts left Wally with a split lip and me with a black eye. Victor came charging around the corner and almost stumbled when he saw who Bogan was holding.

"Good — ! What are *you* two doing here?"

How Wally managed to think of anything to say at a time like that is beyond me, but his conniving mind was still working.

"We had a key. There was one hidden in the barn, it was still there. I bet Les we could sneak in and out without being caught. We just did it for fun."

"Fun? Some fun! Looks like you got your fun, all right," said Victor, taking in our faces.

"They was trying to get away," growled Bogan.

"Where's your uncle?" asked Victor.

"Maybe at my house, but probably home."

Victor jerked his head at Bogan.

"Bring 'em over to the car."

Bogan took us each by an arm and hauled us along. Victor had a phone in his car.

"What's his number?"

Wally told him. He called and got an answer.

"Matt? Victor Ridgway. I'm at the Canby house, and so's your nephew and his buddy You'd better come over. They're in trouble." He was obviously enjoying the chance to give Uncle Matt a headache. "Okay. Make it snappy!"

He hung up and stared at us with hard eyes and a tight grin on his face.

"Otis taught me a lesson, and you fell for it. Of course, that time I didn't have someone with me to cover the other door. You know, I'm really surprised at you. I didn't think you were dumb enough to do anything this stupid. Your uncle's just going to love this!"

Then his face went ugly as he suddenly leaned forward.

"What were you after in there? What did you take? Don't tell me you just went in there for kicks!"

Bogan's grip went hard on our arms as we shrank back.

"But — but we did!"

"Baloney!"

His eyes bored into us. After a moment Wally shrugged.

"Well, okay, we were looking for a puzzle book."

"A puzzle book?"

"Your uncle and Otis worked on a puzzle together that last night —"

"How do you know that?"

"Uncle Matt told us."

"Oh? I guess he tells you too much," sneered Victor. "So where's the puzzle book? Let's see it."

"We couldn't find it. We thought it would be in the desk, but it wasn't."

"Why did you want it?"

"Well, your uncle wrote a word in it for Otis, and we wanted to see what it was. We think it was something that told Otis where the safe was with the gold in it."

Victor stared at us again.

"You mean, you took the chances you did just for *that?*"

"We didn't think we were taking much of a chance," I said, wishing I could give Bogan a look but not quite daring to. As it was I got a shake and a growl from him and some sparkling repartee.

"Oh, yeah? Think yer smart, don'tcha?"

"Well, we got in all right," said Wally.

"You sure did," said Victor, and turned his hard

eyes on Bogan, who wilted noticeably. Then, before we had to try to think of anything else to say, Uncle Matt barreled into Old Farm Road. He screeched to a stop, jumped out, and came toward us with a look that was enough to break our hearts.

"Victor. What's up?"

"Got a breaking-and-entering for you, Matt." Victor was really enjoying himself now. "We caught them trying to sneak out of the house."

"We had a key," said Wally.

"It was still breaking-and-entering," snapped Victor. "Right, Matt?" he asked, and in a dead sort of voice Uncle Matt said, "Right, Victor."

He looked at us, not missing the condition of our faces, but not commenting, either.

"What were you doing in there?"

Wally repeated the story he had given Victor. When he had finished, Victor said,

"So that's it. You take it from here, Matt."

Without looking at us — I guess he couldn't bear to — he said grimly, "I'll book them."

"Not tonight. Let's keep this quiet till after the house is moved. People are going to be here in droves to watch, they're going to have a good time. A thing like this would be bad publicity."

"We'll see," said Uncle Matt. He gave Bogan a level glance that made him drop our arms as if they'd suddenly become red hot. "I'll take them with me. I'm sorry about this, Victor. Goodnight."

"Night, Matt. I'm sorry, too," said Victor, without looking it.

We didn't say goodnight to anybody. We just marched away behind Uncle Matt to his car.

We got into the front seat beside him. He turned into Salem Road and drove along slowly for a block or so before he even spoke. Then, without looking at us:

"All right. What have you got to say?"

"We've got plenty to say, Uncle Matt," said Wally. "We've done three or four things I suppose we had no business doing — we've been wise guys, I guess — we should have told you about them before now, but the thing is, nothing we've found out added up to anything at all until just now, when we were in the house."

"That's right," I said. "You've got to believe us, we're almost sure we're right."

"You can book us or do anything else you want to," said Wally, "but all we ask is, first, *listen* to us!"

Uncle Matt drove on for a while without saying a word. When we came to Wally's house, he pulled into the drive, stopped, and turned off the engine. Then, finally, he turned and looked at us.

"All right. Let's hear it."

15

THE HOUSE-MOVING NEXT
morning drew the kind of crowd that had been expected. We weren't among those who gathered in
front of the house, but they included all our parents,
Shapley Hobson and Ernest Beemis, and the Murphys. A big truck was coupled to the rig, and a
cheer went up as the old house began slowly to move
into Old Farm Road on its way to the Village. A
police car led the way. Ordinarily Uncle Matt
would have been riding in it, but not that morning
Instead, he was sitting in another police car parked
on Salem Road a block from the corner.

The house had hardly cleared the yard before
two dump trucks came down the hill on Old Farm
Road and turned in across the backyard. Victor and

a couple of workmen stood waiting. Victor motioned to the first truck to turn and back in toward the cellar hole.

"Just like he said," grunted Uncle Matt.

The night before he had eventually telephoned Victor to tell him he had released us in our parents' custody for the moment, and in the course of conversation had asked when Victor planned to start filling the cellar hole.

"Right away. The minute the house is gone. No sense wasting time," said Victor.

So now Uncle Matt waited till the first dump truck had made its turn and then said, "Okay, Eddie, let's go."

One of his best men, Eddie Soares, was driving. Wally and I were in the back seat.

Eddie turned onto the lawn, cut across, and stopped near the cellar hole. While Victor watched with a heavy frown, we all got out and walked around to where he was standing. His voice grated as he said, "What are you doing here, Matt? And these kids? I thought —"

"Victor, they *did* find something in the house, something that means we've got to do some digging here before you fill."

At a moment when his nerves were stretched to the breaking point, when he was minutes away from the perfect murder, the sight of the police cruiser coming his way must have been a terrible jolt. Chief Brenner's words completed the one-two punch that cracked his self-control.

"What? You think I'm going to let two trucks wait while you poke around in that muck down there? You're crazy! What do they think you're going to find — gold?"

"No," said Uncle Matt. His voice was sad but very firm. "Not gold. Victor, we're going to have to dig."

With that Victor simply went berserk. He threw himself at us, all of us, and it took everyone plus a couple of the workmen to finally bring him down and under control. Wally and I tried to help, and had new bruises to prove it when it was all over.

I shouldn't have said murder. It wasn't murder, it was manslaughter, the way Victor Ridgway told it, and later on a jury believed him.

The minute the Murphys phoned him that night he suspected what Otis was up to. Victor knew his uncle had a wall safe, he knew where it was, and he even knew the combination, though of course he lied about that later on to Uncle Matt. Several years earlier, his uncle had given him the combination — "so that someone will have it, in case anything happens to me." No doubt it amused the old man to give it to Victor, knowing full well he would never leave anything valuable in it.

Victor walked down through the woods and watched the Murphys leave. As soon as they were gone he entered the house and hid in the guest room across from his uncle's bedroom.

Shortly after nine o'clock Otis Fournier let himself in by way of the back door. Victor stood listening behind the door of the guest room, expecting to hear Otis go into his uncle's room, but heard him enter the next room instead.

Victor eased the door open a crack and waited to see what Otis would come out with. He didn't want to collar his cousin until he knew what it was he was after. He felt pretty sure it would be gold.

He heard a scraping sound — *Fishing Boats in the North Sea* being taken down, no doubt — heard Otis chuckle excitedly and start muttering things like, "Good old Uncle!" and "Ah, me proud beauties!" — this accompanied by the clink of coins.

Victor thought about all the chores and errands he had done for his uncle all his life, and how only a few hours earlier that day he had learned that none of his uncle's millions, none of his money, was being left to him. And now his uncle had put what was probably a fortune in gold in the hands of a nephew who had given him nothing but grief.

When Victor stepped out into the hall he was raging mad. Otis was just coming out of Mrs. Canby's room. He was carrying a large green felt bag. He took one frightened look at Victor and yanked a small revolver out of his pocket. Victor slapped it away and grabbed Otis by the throat. A lifetime of hatred put a red mist in front of his eyes.

When it cleared away his thick fingers had left ridges in Otis's throat, and Otis was not breathing anymore.

In his first moments of panic Victor almost called the police and gave himself up. But then he got to thinking about the gold, all that gold nobody else knew about. He would have to give that up, too.

He put his mind to work, and thought he saw a brilliant way out of the whole mess.

The reason he had suspected Otis right away was that he had been toying with the idea of having a look in the safe himself!

Now, first off, he took a quick look at Mrs. Canby's room but saw nothing that would tell him — or anyone else — where the gold had been hidden. The room was in perfect order. He wondered where Otis had found the gold, but he didn't stop to make a search, because there was no point in it now, and he had too many other things to do.

He hurried into his uncle's room, opened the safe, and was disappointed to find nothing of value in it. He removed the few papers it held and wiped off any fingerprints he might have put on it. Next he opened the desk and strewed papers around to make it look as if Otis had rummaged through it, looking for the safe combination.

He took a gold coin out of the bag and planted it under the bed. He wiped off the frame of the Faithful Shepherd Dog engraving, took it into the hall, pressed Otis's fingerprints on its edges, then laid it on the bed. After that . . .

I have never enjoyed thinking about the next hour or so in the Canby house. Victor carrying the body down to the cellar. Victor taking up duckboards and digging for dear life — his life — in that soft, damp soil. Victor sweating and straining, his heart pounding every time he thought he heard a car slow down or stop outside. Not every man could dig a grave in that short a time, but Victor knew how to handle a shovel, and Victor was powerful, and Victor had motivation, all the motivation he needed.

He did the job, smoothed out the dirt, and put the duckboards in place. When he finished it would have been hard to tell that any digging had taken place there. Later on he had plenty of chances to be alone in the cellar and improve on his job until nobody could have told the earth had recently been disturbed. He hid the gold in an old woodbox that was moldering away in a dark corner. and took it home two days later.

Using the kitchen phone, he called the Peabody Inn and told the Murphys to come home. That done, he was ready to call the police and report a robbery. This was necessary, of course, to set up a reason for Otis's staying out of sight in the future.

He was dialing the police station when he saw us in the backyard. At first he felt trapped. We were obviously coming to the house, heading for the back door. What would he say to us? But then he remembered Wally was Uncle Matt's nephew, and decided he could make good use of us. And it almost worked

Sometimes we wish we'd never got mixed up in the whole business at all. It brought us nothing but grief.

From our parents:

"How are we ever going to be able to trust you two again? When we think of the things you did —!"

From Uncle Matt:

"Sure, you came up with something, and we can thank you for that — but I want to tell you, if ever I catch you sticking your noses into police matters again, you're going to wish you'd never —"

And from Hobby:

"Yes, yes, we certainly do have a new star attraction, and it will be wonderful if the courts do decide the Village is the rightful owner of all that gold — but I can't pretend to be altogether pleased when the first thing that every visitor who comes here now wants to do is have a tour of 'the Murder House'!"

He shuddered, and shook his head sadly. "To think that's what it's called — 'the Murder House'!"

It was almost enough to make us cream our Yamakuras! However, Wally tried to be philosophical about it.

"Well, anyway, we were right."

"Well, yes, finally," I agreed. "You were wrong when you had grave doubts, but we were right when we had grave suspicions!"

THE END